MERLIN'S

THE FOOTNAIL SERIES – BOOK 3

REVELATION

A.K. HOWARD

Merlin's Revelation

ISBN (Paperback): 978-1-990678-13-4

ISBN (Ebook): 978-1-990678-12-7

PROLOGUE

CONSTANTINOPLE, 327 A.D.

The damp, musty smell of soil and earth clung to Queen Helena's nostrils like it had a will of its own. She took a deep breath as she steadied herself, trying not to put too much weight on the wooden bannister beside her.

Constantly trekking up and down the short flight of steps leading to her hidden dungeon was taking its toll on her aged bones. Well, it wasn't exactly a dungeon; more of a room that had been converted into a holding cell for prisoners.

Helena wondered what her son, Emperor Constantine the Great, would say if he knew she had a prisoner tucked away in her secret prison. He would want to know everything, and the truth would be too fantastical for him to entertain. She wouldn't believe herself either.

Who would believe in immortals and magic?

Who would accept that there were individuals who held such power, power that dwarfed the might of kings and queens?

Ever since she had found the cross and the three nails used to crucify Jesus Christ, her reality had become filled with danger and worry. Some nights, she wondered what her life would be like if she hadn't found the powerful relics.

Would the accursed be after her now? Probably not. But then they would have their hands on the nails, and Helena couldn't begin to fathom a world in which the accursed had that kind of that power.

She took another deep breath and continued down the rickety stairs, trying not to wrinkle her nose at the earthy smell.

When she reached the bottom, she walked up to the Praetorian guard blocking the door ahead and gave him a brief nod. He quietly touched his chest with his right fist in acknowledgement.

"How is he this morning?"

"The same as every other morning, Your Highness."

"Open the door."

The guard nodded and turned the lock on the door.

Helena usually tried her best to remember the names of the men risking their lives for her safety, but with all that had been happening, she couldn't recall this guard's name. His face stuck in her mind—she had definitely seen him before—but he was one of many who surrounded her and answered to her personal bodyguard. The guard looked unassuming in his dark brown leather uniform and short sword sheathed by his side, but she wasn't deceived. She had seen the Praetorian guards in combat; they were deadly.

The thick wooden door creaked as it swung open.

The smell of moist earth and body odour grew overwhelming as Helena walked in and glanced around the small, bare cell. What need was there for amenities when you planned on treating another human despicably?

In the center of the room lay a man bound in chains. She took in the prisoner's unkept brown hair and slim build, trying not to flinch at the smell of sweat and grime that radiated from him. He raised hate-filled eyes and glared at Helena.

"RELEASE ME."

The words washed over Queen Helena harmlessly, and she sighed. The immortal tried this every time someone entered the prison, and, by now, he should know his words had no effect on her.

"Don't you tire of this, Marius?"

"I will be free from these shackles, Nail Bearer. I will be free, and you will regret keeping me here," he sneered.

"What are the accursed planning, Marius? Do you still plan on overthrowing the emperor?"

Constantinople was embroiled in unrest and bloodshed of late as some members of the senate had attempted an uprising. What the populace didn't know was that the man in chains had been instrumental in the revolution. He was one of the accursed: immortals bent on destroying Queen Helena and capturing the three nails of power.

Marius laughed. "Your son's pitiful rule will crumble, Nail Bearer. You should have handed over the nails like we asked, and maybe this backwater excuse for an empire would have survived."

"So, you admit that you still plan on overthrowing my son?"

"I plan nothing." Marius glared at Helena with hate. "You cannot hope to get an answer from me, woman. I have ruled since long before this sorry—"

The door opened, and a different guard entered, dressed in full uniform with a breastplate and greaves.

"RELEASE ME," Marius commanded.

The guard flinched but merely closed the door behind him, then bowed his head to Helena.

"You shouldn't be here, Your Highness," he said, brushing back a lock of sandy brown hair.

"I can go where I please, Calisto," the queen snapped.

"But your safety is my priority. You know how dangerous the prisoner is."

"He is in chains. What harm could he possibly do?"

Calisto raised an eyebrow.

"You know what I mean. Don't get cheeky with me, young man."

She knew Calisto took her safety seriously and would ignore her orders if he felt they stood in the way of his performance.

"Has he said anything useful?" her guard asked.

"Nothing of value beyond his constant attempts at being freed."

"And you will never get anything from me," Marius snapped. "Your pathetic interrogation is laughable."

Calisto shared the opinion that their current method of interrogation was wasted on one such as Marius. He would have opted for the guards' more traditional approach, but Queen Helena blatantly refused the idea. She ordered that Marius's skin shouldn't be broken in any way. Instead, his hands had been tied, and he was subjected to sleep deprivation and hunger. So far, these methods had not succeeded in extracting any information.

"Again, your highness, if you'd let my guards interro—"

"The answer is no, Calisto. We will not torture Marius."

"I don't think he's going to tell us what we want to know out of the goodness of his heart, if he has one."

"Then think of another way, Calisto," Helena's tone was firm and final.

Marius smirked, eyeing the captain of the guards with contempt.

Calisto sighed. Their options were limited. It seemed they would not be able to do anything but keep him chained up in the prison for eternity.

Helena took one last look at Marius and left the room with Calisto trailing after her. She reached the bottom of the stairs and grimaced, bracing herself for another battle with the unforgiving steps.

Merlin reached out with his senses, trying to locate the source of power he noticed some minutes ago. It had felt dark and malignant, like something foul and not of this plane of existence.

The sun hadn't risen yet, but he could see streaks of gold creeping over the horizon and casting a yellow hue over Constantinople, bringing an end to the cold night.

Save for the occasional labourer heading out, Merlin was completely alone in the quiet morning.

He reached out again. The feeling was faint, barely recognizable, but definitely there. It seemed to emanate from outside the city walls.

Merlin made his way to the north gate, where he had to wait in line with everyone else, mostly farmers, to pass through. He glanced at the soldiers guarding it, hoping he didn't stand out too much in his white robe and gold sash. He had dressed for an audience with the emperor, who had cancelled at the last moment. He was about to head back to his rooms when he'd detected the use of dark magic.

He suspected one of the accursed—Atticus, to be precise—but he needed to be sure. The line grew shorter, and soon Merlin stood before the two guards. He could have walked past them without stopping, but he didn't want to set a precedent that could lead to a security breach—not when one of your enemies had the ability to morph into anyone.

The soldiers looked Merlin over before indicating for him to move on. He continued walking along the path leading from the gate into the farmland north of the city, sending his senses out at regular intervals to get a feel for the power and the direction it was coming from. After a while, he reached a small farmhouse. The power was very strong here. He had arrived at his destination.

Merlin looked around. Except for the sound of a lone goat bleating in the distance, there was an unearthly silence about the place. He reached out gently, checking for a barrier or a containment spell.

Nothing. No spell, no other sound or sign of life.

Growing increasingly wary, he quickly cast a shield over his body. He opened the small wooden gate that led to the farmhouse and walked toward the front door.

He pushed it open slowly.

The smell hit him; the unmistakable, pungent odour of decayed flesh. He stepped carefully into the house, now on high alert. It was dark inside, even though the day was becoming bright and sunny. He heard flies buzzing in the darkness, and beyond that, something else…

Silent whispering; dark, guttural voices whispering words not of this earth. Then, as his eyes adjusted to the gloomy room, Merlin saw the reason for the flies.

In front of him was a circle of dead bodies. A slaughtered goat lay at the center of the circle with a chalk inscription scrawled on the floor around it. Merlin knew an amateurish attempt at a summoning circle when he saw one.

What fools, he thought. *Why would anyone in their right mind want to summon one of the seven princes of hell?*

The inscription on the floor was wrong, and, even if they had gotten it right, he doubted that whoever had done this would have had the spiritual power and will to command a prince of hell.

But had they managed to open a gateway between planes?

He couldn't be sure.

Some form of a doorway had definitely been opened; that was clear from the whispers of the dark entities around him. Any normal person that stepped into the room would be driven insane by their presence.

Thankfully, Merlin was no ordinary man.

As the whispering grew louder, he began to cast a spell. The entities were bound to this location and would need a host to move elsewhere. Unfortunately for them, Merlin's will was unbreakable.

He wove light and purity into his spell as he cast. When he released the banishing spell, the room was flooded with light. The entities screamed as it illuminated their dark minds and shattered their hold over the earthly plane.

They were gone.

The darkness in the room receded, and Merlin could now take a closer look at the scene in front of him. There were five bodies arranged around the summoning circle. Their faces all held the same look of horror and anguish, a testament to their last moments before death took them.

Merlin sighed.

He would need to confirm whether the summoning spell had worked or not. He cast another spell, and a small fireball appeared in his palm. With a flick of his wrist, he released the flame. It rolled forward, expanding rapidly before engulfing the bodies.

Merlin walked away from the farm as it burnt to the ground behind him.

"RELEASE ME."

Marius felt the power of his words leave his prison cell and wash over the man outside the door, but it achieved nothing. The guard simply shook the words from his mind before they faded into nothing.

And yet, Marius smiled. The power had reached further than it had the previous day. He was getting stronger.

He had been in this prison for more than two weeks. He counted the passing days by keeping track of the rotation of the guards and the meal they gave him once a day.

They had refused to torture him. Marius sneered at their weakness. The nail bearer thought she could play the righteous act with him. Even so, he knew he was lucky they decided to refrain from breaking his body. He wouldn't have had any hope of resisting their torture; Marius simply couldn't abide physical pain. He knew he would have told them anything they wanted to hear if they had resorted to heated iron rods and three-tonged whips.

"RELEASE ME."

He felt his power surge again, and, this time, it reached the edges of the palace walls.

Marius had been working on sending his power out further and further ever since he was captured. Slowly but surely, the radius of his reach had expanded. He knew he wouldn't be able to affect any of the guards outside his cell; they were all immune to his words of power—something he hadn't known was possible until he had fought the nail bearer. It seemed that anyone who managed to break free from his influence became immune to it. Marius suspected that the guards watching over his cell were the soldiers he'd tangled with before. But what the nail bearer and her flock of impotent stick figures didn't know was that he wasn't really after these guards. His hope was that his words would reach outside the palace walls and connect with someone he could control.

For over two weeks, he had practiced patiently, and now his patience seemed to be bearing fruit. He could afford to wait a little while longer.

Summoning as much power as he could, Marius released his words with an internal scream.

"RELEASE ME!"

The words hit the palace walls and penetrated them, pushing through to the other side. Marius felt exhaustion overwhelm him. He closed his eyes and was about to fall asleep when he felt his words slam into someone. He snapped up as the connection snapped into place.

Yes!

He wove his power around the mind of the person he had captured. He burrowed deep into their consciousness, scattering their pitiful defences and destroying their will. In his hurried desperation, he shattered his captive's mind as he clawed deep into their psyche.

Marius felt no remorse. Escape was within his grasp.

Merlin followed the thin footpath away from the burnt farmhouse. He could sense traces of an ethereal nature all around him. Something or someone that didn't belong here was on this plane. He needed to return to the palace, but he couldn't allow the entity to roam free. He prepared an offensive spell and fortified his shield, hoping that he was wrong. But somehow, he didn't think he would be that lucky.

Merlin had hoped to link the secret cult that was gaining ground in Constantinople to the accursed's attempted insurrection. He considered whether Atticus might have had a hand in the sudden spike in pagan worship and blood sacrifice. The accursed may have instigated more awareness of the supernatural, but the mediocre occult activities had most likely become popular without their influence. Either way, he needed to crush its spread before it consumed the city, or someone released an entity that was too powerful to contain.

An entity like the one he hunted now.

Scouring the area around the footpath, something caught his eye. Blood stained the leaves at the top of a small bush.

The air throbbed and shimmered around him as he cast a tracking spell and released it over the blood, which glowed and expanded, forming a fine red thread that curled upward and then veered into the forest. Now he had a trail to follow. He had to find whatever had spilled its blood here.

He left the footpath and briskly set off after the thread, following it through the thick forest. A few minutes later, he arrived at a clearing in the woods. The large trees surrounding it cast a dark shadow over the space. As his eyes adjusted to the dim light, Merlin spotted a body on the ground a few feet in front of him. The glowing red thread of his spell led straight to it.

He paused.

"You can get on your feet now. I sense you for what you are," Merlin said.

He waited as the body remained unmoving.

Merlin was sure that this was a trap. He reached out with his senses to determine whether there was any magical power coming from the body. Sure enough, he immediately sensed the throbbing of energy.

Whatever was lying before him was strong, but thankfully, it wasn't a prince of hell. The summoning had failed.

The body stirred and slowly got to its feet. It looked like an ordinary man, but Merlin knew better.

"How did you sense my presence, human?" The sound of the entity's voice resounded, seeming to come from everywhere at the same time.

"Nice trick, but I can sense you for what you are."

The possessed man's face twisted as the soul struggled against the presence of the foreign entity. It looked at Merlin and hissed in anger.

"You bear the mark of the Son of the Creator. I have a right to this body. I was summoned here. You cannot cast me out."

"I can and I will. You took advantage of their ignorance and deceived them."

"I will not go," the entity raged.

"I wasn't asking for your permission."

Merlin quickly wove a containment spell and released it, locking the entity within the clearing's boundaries. The possessed man rushed at Merlin with a burst of unnatural speed.

He ducked to avoid the man's swing and spun around to face him as he stumbled. He cast a tendril of air and wrapped it around the man, then channelled the air toward the ground, and the man was jerked backward.

13

"No!" the man raged as he was dragged away.

Merlin was glad that the botched summoning had attracted a lesser demon. While they were strong, they couldn't cast spells or do magic. Things would have been a lot worse if it had been a high demon or a prince of hell. In seconds, Merlin cast four more air spells around the possessed man's limbs, pinning him to the ground.

"Release me," the entity snarled.

"With pleasure."

Merlin formed a ball of light and slammed it into the possessed man's chest. The entity screamed as light flooded the man's body.

The dark form of the entity rose out of the man, and Merlin blasted it away with raw energy. Then he released the spell holding the man, and the now-human body slumped to the ground again. Merlin could feel his heart beating faintly. He was barely alive.

Merlin grimaced. He needed information immediately and couldn't wait for the man to recover.

He gathered another spell, this time one of life and vitality, and released it over the prone figure.

The man jerked, then his eyes snapped open as he took a deep breath. He looked at his surroundings in confusion.

"You are safe from the darkness, stranger," Merlin said, but his words didn't seem to reach the man. He flinched back, and his eyes darted around in fear. Merlin bent down and placed his hand on the man's chest. "Who taught you the spell to summon an entity from the other realm?"

The man focused on Merlin, and he whispered a name faintly.

"Derog the Banisher."

Merlin's eyes widened.

It couldn't be true. It had to be a mistake.

Derog was dead.

Marius's words of power made it possible for him to see through the eyes of the young man he had subverted and control his movements. He steered him into the palace, through the main hall to the kitchen, where he grabbed a tray of food, and down the stairs that led to Marius's cell.

"Halt," the prison guard commanded as he reached him.

Marius compelled the young man to stop.

"What do you have there?" the guard asked.

"Food for the prisoner."

The guard frowned. "It's not time for his meal."

Marius made the young man shrug his shoulders. "I don't know about that," he droned. "The queen told me to bring a plate of food for the prisoner. I am only following orders."

The guard grunted and turned to unlock the cell door. Marius had commanded the young man to tuck a knife underneath the wooden tray, and he struck as soon as it opened.

The guard heard the clatter of the plates and reacted instantly. He leapt aside to evade the attack, but it was not enough. The thrust meant for the guard's heart pierced his ribs instead.

The guard grunted and caught the man's hand in a tight grip. The man snarled and slammed his forehead into the guard's face. The soldier's helmet took the brunt of the blow, but the young man was unrelenting.

Marius's control had overridden any fear of pain. He slammed his head into the guard's face again and again until he fell to the ground.

"Quick, search him for the key," Marius ordered.

Moments later, Marius was free. He rubbed his raw wrists and turned to the young man, who could barely stand. His face was a bloody mess of bone, flesh, and skin.

"Pick up the guard's sword and protect me with your life."

The young man obeyed and waited for Marius's next command.

Marius smiled. For now, he needed to get away, but he would be back. And he would make the empress pay for the time he spent shackled in this cell.

He had timed his escape well. The guards' next shift rotation was not for another hour, giving him enough time to get far away from the palace.

"Lead the way out," Marius commanded.

The young man turned and headed for the short flight of stairs with Marius close behind.

1

Such a simple thing, yet so much power.

Gen Isherwood stared at the nail in her hand. It was six inches long and rusted brown with age. Although it looked ordinary, the nail pulsed with power. Gen could sense the power flowing from it.

There used to be three of them: three nails that bore power from being used in the crucifixion of Jesus Christ.

Now, only one remained.

The foot nail. The most powerful of the three and the one nail that had been in her family for centuries. It was also the source of all the trouble in her life, if she was inclined to look at things that way.

Maybe she would have seen it that way at another time in her life, but not after everything she'd experienced. Not after the visions and the interactions she'd had with the Son of the Creator.

After all she'd seen, it was out of the question to be so petty or think so small.

The fate of the world was literally on her shoulders, and the small piece of metal she held in her hand would play a prominent role in the fight against the darkness. She still occasionally saw visions when she touched the nail, but it was happening less and less now. It was as though she didn't even need to have any physical contact with the nail anymore to have the visions anymore.

She'd grown spiritually. Her ability to tap into her power was proof of that.

Gen leaned back in her chair and drummed her fingers on the kitchen table. It wasn't morning quite yet, but she could see the first traces of sunrise through the kitchen window that looked out at the Triple 7 ranch.

When she was little, the kitchen seemed massive, but now it felt cramped and barely sufficient to contain the number of people living on the ranch.

Not that she was complaining.

Without the others, she would have lost the fight long ago. In fact, she would probably be dead.

Gen rubbed the nape of her neck as she tried to ease the tension in her bones, then tied up her flaming red hair to keep it out of her way. She dropped the nail on the table and spun it. Deep in thought, she watched it go around in circles, whirring as it rotated.

Over the years, many had died for the nails. A battle between good and evil was already raging way before she was born, and then the nail had landed in her lap. The burden of ownership had been handed to her as the next nail bearer.

Gen heard footsteps approaching and looked up as Mark walked into the kitchen.

"You 're up early," Mark said as he headed for the coffee maker by the fridge.

"Couldn't sleep." Gen watched him prepare his cup of coffee.

Mark exuded an air of confidence that Gen found appealing. He wasn't full of himself, but he looked dependable. His dark brown hair and rugged good looks added to his charm, but it was his heart that she had fallen in love with.

"What?" Mark asked as he pulled up a seat and flopped into it. The chair creaked under the mass of firm muscle as Mark adjusted to a comfortable position.

"Nothing. Just admiring the view."

The corner of Mark's lips curled up in amusement, and Gen felt her face flush.

What was it about him that made her giddy like a teenager with a crush?

She cleared her throat and turned her attention back to the foot nail, now still on the table. She tried to block out the sound of Mark sipping his coffee, hoping to keep her thoughts focused on the nail rather than on her protector.

But she could feel his eyes on her, and her heart decided to betray her again.

"Stop that." Gen looked up to see that wicked smile still plastered on his face.

"What?" Mark asked innocently.

"Stop staring. I can feel you ogling me." Gen tried to feign annoyance, and Mark laughed at her silly attempt.

"Ogling. That's a new one. Where did you get that from? Wait, let me guess. Myrddin?"

Gen laughed. "Who else? Sometimes I think he gets carried away and reverts to ancient English."

"What's wrong, Gen?" he asked after a brief pause.

"Why would you ask that?"

Mark raised an eyebrow, and Gen smiled ruefully. She didn't know if it was because he was her protector, but Mark always seemed to be able to read her.

"Don't know. Can't really say, but I'm kind of restless."

Mark nodded in understanding. "It sometimes happens with soldiers, in between missions when they have nothing to do. You just have to try to appreciate the peaceful times."

"Okay."

She understood his point, but she still couldn't relax. She couldn't say why, but deep down, she sensed something approaching. Something they needed to be ready for.

"I should be the one worrying," he said with a smile.

"It's more than that, Mark. It's been too peaceful. Something's coming."

He set down his cup and focused all his attention on Gen. She felt his piercing gaze settle on her, and her heartbeat fluttered uneasily for a second. Mark could sense magic, or the use of what they had come to call 'essence', the part of the human soul that could channel power.

As his gaze washed over her, the pressure vanished.

"What did you do?" Gen asked. She was slightly shaken but managed to keep her breath steady.

"Checked to see if you were being influenced by an external force. You 're clean."

"Good to know."

"Can you explain the feeling you're having?"

She nodded with a smile. That was another reason she loved the man sitting across from her: He never doubted her, and his belief in her gave her the strength to believe in herself. Gen took the nail in her hand and rubbed its surface as she gathered her thoughts.

"You know in one of those scary movies when the character is in the room with the killer? Everything looks okay, but the person can sense danger even if they can't see it. Danger is coming, Mark. I can sense it."

He reached out and clasped her hand in his. The determined look on his face relaxed her.

Whatever was coming, they would be ready.

Russell Patel turned the key in the lock and twisted the knob to open the door of his studio. Calling it a studio was a stretch, but it was what it was. The small space had once just served for storage, and it could barely contain the small desk and bed that now took up most of the room.

Russell tried not to let his frustration get the better of him as he dropped a handful of letters on the desk next to his computer. He needed to get his act together, or he would end up on the street. He could hear his father's laughter echoing in the back of his mind. He knew what the old man would say if Russell got tossed out for failing to pay his rent.

Come to beg your washed-out old man for a place to stay, loser?

You will always be a failure, kid.

Not that Russell was a kid anymore. Life had just been unfair to him, taking great delight in sucker punching him again and again. He knew he had what it takes to rise to greatness, but he had never had a chance to excel.

What did others have that he didn't? He was smart and hardworking. His friends were all making it in their respective fields, and even though he had graduated from university with a much higher GPA than his peers, he was the one now living in a shoe box and trying to make ends meet with his podcasts, broadcasting the trash his clients wanted.

Where had he gone wrong?

He grimaced as his father's laughter echoed in his mind. He shut the door behind him and switched on the computer. The monitor flickered, and the familiar whine of the CPU coming to life calmed his nerves. His office chair bumped against the wall as he pulled it out, and he had to squeeze his slim, lanky body into the space between it and the desk to maneuver into the leather seat.

He had found the chair at a pawn shop and had paid for it by helping the owner with a computer issue, as well as cleaning his dog's stinking cage. The fat, bald twit working there had taken advantage of his desperation.

But Russell got even.

He had built quite a followership for his podcast in Saskatoon; it seemed people listened to what he had to say. Telling everyone about the crooked pawn shop dealer that operated in stolen goods had been satisfying.

Russell had no qualms about lying and probably ruining somebody's business. That was life.

If you relaxed your guard, life was sure to sucker punch you, and Russell believed in giving out as much as he got.

As he waited for the computer to come to life, he picked up the envelopes and sorted through them. They were mostly overdue bills and notices from the stuck-up landlady, but the last envelope caught his attention.

He didn't recognize the sender's name or address. When he tore it open, a flash drive fell into his palm, and a small piece of paper flitted to the floor. He bent down to pick it up and frowned as he read the short note.

"Enough with the lies."

Interesting.

His curiosity piqued, Russell quickly inserted the

flash drive into his computer's USB port. The folder that popped up contained a video clip and a text file. He opened the video without hesitation.

He could tell that the video was recorded on a phone; the quality wasn't great. The footage showed a young woman with red hair bending over a little girl on the sidewalk of a quiet street. Russell couldn't make out what she was saying, but there was a gasp from the little girl.

"Mum, I don't feel the pain anymore," the little girl said.

Russell watched in silence as a seemingly miraculous event unfolded on the screen. He looked at the piece of paper again.

The clip must have been doctored. He felt anger rise within him. He had sought the help of one of these so-called televangelists once. They were all fakes and deserved to be exposed for what they really were.

Next, he clicked on the other file. It was a dossier on someone called Genesis Isherwood. The picture at the top of the document showed the same woman from the video.

He grinned maliciously as he opened his podcasting app and pulled the tabletop microphone closer.

Time to put a stop to this farce.

Mark gripped his wooden sword tightly as he studied his opponent. He blocked out all other sounds and concentrated on the man standing before him.

He needed total focus if he was going to win the fight with Lucilius. Even though the man wasn't an immortal anymore, Lucilius still had years of experience going for him.

But Mark had a means of countering that advantage; he could draw from a well of information from previous protectors.

The pair sparred most mornings, an arrangement they'd come to when Mark saw Lucilius training alone next to the barn one morning. The early morning sessions kept them in shape and created the type of bond that only came through fighting together. At least, that was Mark's hope.

He noticed Lucilius's left foot move forward a fraction, a clear sign he was preparing to attack. Sure enough, Lucilius leapt forward with a vicious thrust. Though they were sparring with wooden swords, Mark had no doubt that such an attack could still skewer the unwary. Lucilius was fast, even without any power to rely on, but Mark parried the thrust to the side. He didn't return the attack yet, as he could see that Lucilius wasn't quite done; the first strike had only been a feint.

He deflected the next two strikes, too. He could feel the air ripple next to his cheek as the wooden sword jabbed inches from his face.

The fight became a frenzy as Lucilius swung left and right, each time encountering Mark's sword. Mere months ago, he wouldn't have been able to block these strikes, but things had changed.

Mark had changed.

He grinned as he felt the rhythm of the battle resonate within him. Images flooded his mind unbidden, and his body began to react from pure muscle memory.

He leaned back as Lucilius's sword again cut the air inches from his face. They were both wearing padded armour but had opted to leave their faces unprotected, Mark because he didn't like the restriction of a helmet, and Lucilius because Mark had refused one.

Mark stepped forward as his opponent's sword completed its arc, leaving Lucilius with no room to strike again.

Confident that the odds were now in his favour, Mark swung at his exposed side, expecting to make contact, but to his surprise, his strike met with empty air.

Lucilius had shifted his weight at the last moment, and Mark's advantage had become a huge disadvantage. He was caught completely off-balance, watching as Lucilius came at him with a thrust aimed straight at his chest.

But he reacted immediately, and the sword only brushed the side of his ribs as he sailed up into the air. Lucilius's grin turned into shock as Mark twisted into a somersault, thrusting at his chest mid-air.

It hit Lucilius's padded chest and threw him backward. Mark ended the somersault by landing on his feet, and he watched in surprise as Lucilius staggered and fell backward.

The sound of clapping brought them back to the

world, and he turned to see Gen, Josephine, and Isabella standing on the porch, cheering them on.

"What the heck just happened?" Isabella asked in surprise.

"They were moving too fast for me to see most of it, but that last move was—amazing!" Josephine answered, her cheeks flushed with excitement.

Mark saw a worried look cross Gen's face as he walked toward Lucilius, who was slowly getting to his feet. He could understand her concern. He felt it too. Although he was holding his wooden sword loosely, he was prepared for anything.

Lucilius had once been one of the strongest men to walk the earth. Such a move would have been unable to hurt him months ago.

Now, he was mortal. Gen had played a pivotal role in Lucilius's redemption, and Mark couldn't help but wonder if he resented losing his powers.

"You cheated," Lucilius rasped as he rubbed his chest.

Mark studied him carefully, trying to gauge his feelings. Lucilius had always been the silent type, his brooding personality very similar to Mark's.

"I didn't cheat."

"You used your powers, even though we agreed no powers while sparring."

Mark paused, then shook his head. "I don't have any powers, Lucilius."

"Then you delude yourself," he snorted.

"Are you okay, Lucilius?" Gen said, walking over and looking worried as she glanced between the two.

"Your protector cheats, Nail Bearer. He uses powers in a sparring match."

"And I told him I don't have powers," Mark objected.

Gen raised an eyebrow and tried not to smile.

"What?" Mark studied the knowing look on Gen's face, confused.

"You can sense magic, Mark. You have the wisdom of countless generations of fighters. Do I have to go on?" Gen's smile remained, and Mark found himself returning it.

"When you put it like that—"

Mark turned to Lucilius and extended his hand. "I'm sorry if it seemed that way, Lucilius. It wasn't intentional."

Lucilius gripped Mark's hand in a firm handshake, and Mark winced internally. He nodded in understanding when he saw the look of appreciation in Gen's eyes.

Lucilius was in a place where he felt unsure of himself and his position in the group—not that the ex-immortal would ever admit that. But Mark could relate. He had felt useless fighting Lucilius when he was still an accursed.

The first time, Lucilius had pinned Mark to a bed with a sword through the torso. Only the timely intervention of Gen's grandfather had saved him.

The second time was worse—Mark had died.

Lucilius had driven his sword through his chest, killing him before Gen revived him.

Now, their one-time enemy was a member of their budding family.

That would be hard for any sane person to wrap their head around, but here they were. Gen had a big heart, a heart that seemed capable of forgiving anyone.

Mark went along with her wishes, and though he could say that he no longer hated Lucilius, he didn't see himself adopting an open-arms policy when it came to the former immortal.

"You guys are simply out of this world." Josephine rushed to Lucilius's side with a wide grin plastered on her face.

Her shaven head and slim, frail body spoke of her miserable struggle with cancer, which would have been terminal if she hadn't been healed—a miracle made possible by Gen's powers. The same night Gen dragged Mark's soul back from the great beyond, Josephine was healed too.

Mark watched Lucilius head back to the house with Josephine tagging along.

"What's with those two?" he asked Gen, who shrugged in response.

"Don't have an answer for you, but whatever it is, I'm glad Josephine is so willing to forgive and forget."

She glanced at him as she spoke.

"What? I've forgiven him too."

"Only forgiven him?"

"You know he ran me through with his sword—twice?"

"I know Mark, but he's changed."

"That's why he's still here with us, Gen. If I still had even an iota of suspicion that all this was an act..."

He gritted his teeth and turned to stare after Lucilius. He had a responsibility to keep Gen safe, and nothing would stop him from doing just that.

2

Benedict Callaway tried to steady his trembling hands.

It wouldn't do for anyone to see that he was scared. He adjusted his glasses and snuck a quick glance at his colleagues working committedly at their workstations.

Benedict's desk was one of four in the large lab he worked in every day to analyze data and make predictions based on those analyses.

The work was simple and mostly boring, but the data that had arrived at his workstation four days ago was frightening. Benedict couldn't believe that anyone would justify risking countless human lives for the sake of making a profit.

He knew how the world worked, and he had managed to numb his conscience over the years while working behind this desk, but there had to be a line that no one should cross.

Benedict didn't mind that he would be labeled a traitor. The lives of millions of people were at stake. He was willing to face whatever punishment he would incur by telling the world what was happening at Amber Corporations.

None of his colleagues were paying him any attention as the progress bar on his monitor creep slowly past the 50% mark.

What if he was caught before the download finished?

He glanced at the security guard stationed outside the lab and tried to still his jittery left leg and silence his shoe tapping on the tile floor. His white lab coat trailed on the floor as he leaned closer to the monitor, willing the download to speed up. He ran his hand through his bushy hair in agitation as it reached 75%.

He was definitely going to be caught.

Benedict snuck another glance at the security guard, and this time, the guard looked his way. He turned away quickly, noticing the guard frown from the corner of his eye.

I'm dead.

He wasn't a hero. He should have left things the way they were. Now, he would be arrested, or worse, killed for trying to be something he wasn't.

The beeping sound of a key card indicated that the lab's glass door was activating. It slid silently open. He had to look up; he couldn't help himself. The security guard was heading toward his workstation, watching him closely.

The guard's arrival got the others' attention, and

the whole room stopped what they were doing to watch what was unfolding.

Benedict looked at his monitor, feeling light-headed with apprehension. The download bar was at 92%. He needed to do something, and so he did the first thing that came to his mind: he got to his feet and started dancing.

Humming Michael Jackson's *Thriller*, he tried unsuccessfully to imitate the legend's iconic moves. His rapidly beating heart slowed as the guard stopped walking to watch Benedict make a fool of himself. His colleagues started clapping, some waving their hands in support of his antics. Benedict twisted his legs and grabbed his crotch, now fully committed to the distraction he was creating.

"What the hell is going on here?"

Benedict froze, his right hand still pressed against his crotch as he stared into Amy Glover's eyes. The lab immediately descended into a hushed silence as Benedict tried to compose himself.

"Will somebody tell me what the blazes is going on here? And why are you dancing, Doctor Callaway?"

Amy Glover was an average five foot six, but nevertheless, Benedict took an involuntary step back. She could be quite intimidating, and the scowl on her face told Benedict that his job hung in the balance.

His dancing antics may have prevented the guard from seeing what he was doing, but Benedict could still lose his job.

"Just relieving some stress, Doctor Glover. I like to dance when I need to be creative."

"You are a scientist, Doctor Callaway. Why would you need to be creative?"

Why indeed? Benedict thought with a grimace.

Amy walked over and peered at his monitor. The screensaver displayed a twisting, amoebic pattern. She reached out, about to tap the keyboard.

Benedict was surprised that the security guard standing by his side couldn't hear his heart pounding in his chest. He felt faint, and sweat matted his hair on his forehead as Doctor Glover's finger hovered over the space bar key.

Then Benedict heard a buzzing sound. Doctor Glover reached into her white lab coat and extracted a cellphone.

"Yes?" She listened for a minute before turning around and heading for the door. Benedict breathed a sigh of relief he didn't know he'd bottled up.

The guard was still standing next to him, fidgeting, clearly unsure what to do, until Benedict raised an eyebrow at him, and he trudged back to his post outside the lab.

Dismissing his colleagues' questions with a wave of his hand, Benedict got back to work. He tapped a key on his keyboard, and his monitor turned back on, revealing the folder he'd been transferring. He quickly closed it and ejected a memory card, then unstrapped his wristwatch and opened its bottom casing. The tiny memory card fit perfectly over the ticking gears and was hidden as he snapped the metal casing back into place.

Now, he only had to walk through the metal detectors at the exit without the card setting them off.

Myrddin tried to act as natural among the crowd of people waiting for the auction to start. Wearing a black tuxedo and pencil-thin trousers, his white hair cut short and beard trimmed, he certainly looked the part. He held himself with an air of arrogance that only the wealthy and powerful could pull off—a true aristocrat.

The wizard had cast a glamour over himself to render his face forgettable. People would look at him and see someone else: still a well-dressed, middle-aged man, but with slightly different features.

His nose appeared somewhat more prominent, his eyes browner. His cheekbones sat higher on his face to sell the look of one with European heritage. Gen would have been surprised at how naturally the role came to him, how perfectly he blended in with the crowd. Once, he had walked the corridors of power, and, as for material wealth, that he truly did have. After all, he was centuries old, ensuring the one ingredient that invariably brought wealth—time.

Myrddin looked around casually, wondering if the location was secure enough.

Security was tight.

In each corner of the room, armed men in combat suits straddled automatic rifles. No one seemed bothered by their presence. The people in the room weren't your average Mr. and Mrs. Jones; this was not the place for soccer mums or sales dads. These were crooked individuals of the underworld, and Myrddin wouldn't have been surprised if most of them were also armed to the teeth.

He sat down in one of the rows of chairs and waited for the auction to start.

About a week ago, Myrddin had received an email informing him of an item that the sender believed he would be very interested in. Years earlier, when he was after the other two nails of power, he had sent a chain of commands into the world to ensure that his alter ego, an unscrupulous businessman with an interest in ancient artifacts, would be notified if anything surfaced that fit his specifications.

He was surprised when he received an invitation to attend this underground auction where, the message hinted, he would perhaps find what he had been searching for. He couldn't ignore such an opportunity and had travelled to Italy to participate in the auction.

He fidgeted with his collar as he stopped himself from scratching an itch on the side of his neck. The damn tuxedo was too tight, but it seemed that was the trending fashion amongst the wealthy and powerful. That, and the ability to suffer in silence.

He could have used a spell to alter the fabric of the suit or even loosen it somehow, but he didn't know if there was anyone present who could detect magic. Better to suffer in silence than expose himself.

The auctioneer walked up to the podium and rapped his gavel.

"Good evening, ladies and gentlemen. Without wasting time, we'll start the auction with this ancient relic, a pair of slippers believed to have been worn by Queen Cleopatra. The opening bid starts at two hundred thousand dollars. Do I hear two hundred thousand?"

Hands raised until the shoes were finally sold for two hundred and eighty thousand dollars.

Item after item was brought out and auctioned off. Myrddin was sure to raise his card from time to time, but he didn't win any bids. So far, nothing was of any interest to him, and he was beginning to wonder if he'd wasted his time.

"The final item tonight is the crown of thorns believed to have been worn by Jesus Christ the Messiah."

Myrddin's eyes snapped up to the auction block.

A young woman in a lavish evening gown walked across the stage carrying a glass case containing a wreath of thin, intertwining branches.

Could it be the real thing?

If it was, he would have to make sure it didn't get into the wrong hands.

Candice Blackburn gripped her bidding card tightly, trying to suppress her anger.

She couldn't believe what was happening.

They had a deal. The auction house had promised not to publicly sell the crown, but it seemed they had no sense of honour.

Raging inwardly but maintaining her calm demeanour, Candice tucked an errant blonde lock behind her ear and glanced around the room. Everyone seemed poker-faced and indifferent, but she could feel the excitement all around her.

This was the item they had all been waiting for.

Some people shifted in their seats, unable to mask their anticipation. Others did much better. Candice noticed an elderly man in a black tux who was waiting calmly in his seat for the auctioneer to begin. The man didn't fidget or give away any other tells. He looked bored as their eyes met, but Candice wasn't deceived.

She smoothed her gown and turned her attention back to the auctioneer. There was nothing she could do at the moment. She'd have to deal with the cheaters later.

"We will be starting this bid at one million dollars," the auctioneer said with a smile.

The gasps of outrage from some bidders relaxed her a little. One million was twice what she'd offered to pay for the crown of thorns; there wouldn't be any takers at that amount.

But then, a woman in an elegant, glittering black dress raised her card, and Candice's heart sank.

"Do I hear one point one million?"

Another hand went up, and Candice felt like burning the place down.

And she could. She wasn't just any run-of-the-mill wealthy antiquarian.

She had power—real power.

Candice controlled her anger and held up her card when the auctioneer raised the bid to one million and five hundred thousand dollars.

Myrddin was watching the auction with keen interest. He noticed the petite blonde bid one and a half million and grimaced. He was certain no one else would go any higher than his one point four million dollar bid, but he was wrong.

It seemed the blonde lady wanted the crown as well, but did she know its significance?

Myrddin chanted silently and slowly rotated his right index finger.

A tendril of a spell whirled around his digit, and he directed it toward the glass case.

The spell was barely noticeable, devoid of real power, and it would go completely undetected unless another very powerful caster was present. It penetrated the glass case with no resistance and settled on the wreath of thorns. Within seconds, the spell dissipated, but it told Myrddin what he needed to know.

"Going at one point five million—once, twice... sold."

The auctioneer's gavel struck the auction block. The crown of thorns now belonged to the pretty young blonde.

Myrddin watched the woman rise to her feet and exit the room. Another item, a piece of the remains of a lost king, was called out, but Myrddin wasn't paying attention.

The blonde woman reached the doors and looked back for a moment. Myrddin locked eyes with her for a second, and then the woman was gone.

Myrddin frowned. For a moment, the woman had exuded power—enough power for him to sense.

It had almost felt like she was letting him know that he wasn't the only one with power in the room, and that could only mean that she'd been able to sense his spell. And if she had, did she know that the item she just paid for was a fake?

Benedict slipped the wristwatch into the manila envelope and licked the adhesive strip. He sealed the envelope, flipped it over, and wrote down an address.

His sitting room was small and overlooked the ugly street below. He had always dreamed of having a sea view but working in the city meant having an apartment surrounded by concrete and iron.

Benedict smoothed the letter, feeling a twinge of guilt as he realized that he could be bringing trouble to the recipient's doorstep. Unfortunately, he couldn't think of any other person he could trust within his tiny circle of friends.

Not that the recipient was a friend. They'd attended the same university, though Benedict had been three years ahead. But he had seen the recipient's heart: always ready to help others and make sacrifices.

Hopefully, the recipient still possessed those qualities because, truth be told, Benedict himself was selfish.

He should have spoken out months ago but was thinking only of self-preservation. He hoped it wasn't too late to redeem himself.

Amber Corporation couldn't be allowed to get away with what they were planning.

Deep in thought, Benedict didn't see the black sedan parked across from his apartment nor the two men inside watching him.

3

O' Neal's mind was swirling with a thousand different possibilities and outcomes. He sat with his head tilted to the side, his eyes glazed over. Unaware of his surroundings, he struggled to decipher the random images that flooded his mind.

He had been going crazy ever since he'd received his gift; ever since Gen opened his heart and mind to the possibility of magic and the power of the crucifixion nail.

O'Neal remembered his vision when he'd touched Gen's hands. He had always been skeptical of things that couldn't be explained logically. Being a doctor made him cynical about fairy tales and what people called "faith." He'd had a hard time believing that the supernatural was real, even when Myrddin had teleported him out of danger when Lucilius and Remus came to the hospital to kill him. His rational mind tried to make sense of what had happened, and when that failed, he did what any reasonable person would do—he had filed the incident away and blocked it from his thoughts.

Maybe that was why he was given this gift? Now he saw the truth of all things. When Gen had held his hands and transported him through time, he saw the crucifixion of Jesus of Nazareth.

What he once doubted had played out before him, and he came back from the experience changed.

He saw things differently.

Life as a doctor seemed like eons ago now. He was myopic and blind to the real world, just helping patients when he could and acknowledging the limitations of science.

Not anymore.

These thoughts swirled in his head, along with a mass of visions and images. If he hadn't found a way to create compartments in his mind, he would have long been broken by the deluge of information he was constantly receiving.

These days he barely slept, and time seemed to work differently for him now that he could see so many endless paths and outcomes.

He was in a race to save his sanity, and he was barely managing. But victory seemed possible. Like the breaking dawn after a long and dark night, the library he had built in his subconscious mind held a promise of sanity. That's where O'Neal stacked away the countless images that constantly poured into his mind unbidden.

Once he mastered filing the images away in real time, he would be more productive and useful to the group. He might even get back a semblance of a normal life if he could learn to keep up with the influx of information.

When the demon Asmodeus attacked the ranch, O'Neal's mind was drowning in possibilities. He couldn't keep up with the random images that bombarded his senses.

That night could have ended in a million possible ways. O'Neal was glad for the present outcome: they won; they were all alive to tell the tale.

Somehow, he was now also able to read magic and tweak it. Not to the extent that it would become something new, as such, but O'Neal could make another person's magic *better.* This ability had come in handy when Asmodeus opened a portal to hell in the center of Dundurn. Josephine needed to reverse time to prevent it from happening, and he had been able to pinpoint the exact moment that would lead to a win for the group.

O'Neal filed the last image in its appropriate compartment, and his eyes grew clear. Suddenly, he was back in the here and now.

He lifted his head and looked around. He was in the sitting room of the ranch house, with Isabella on the sofa across from him. O'Neal stopped the myriad download of possibilities that came from merely glancing in her direction. He refused to be swallowed by the flood anymore.

Isabella looked up from the tablet on her lap, and their eyes met. She smiled uncertainly, not sure whether O'Neal was really present in the conscious world.

He smiled back and saw her eyes widen in surprise.

"Guys!" she shouted.

O'Neal took a moment to appreciate the person smiling at him. Isabella had ash-blonde hair that fell to her shoulders, and he could smell a faint trace of lavender soap. Images rushed in; O'Neal couldn't stop the flow. He gritted his teeth as he struggled to push them aside.

Focus! he willed his mind.

He would not be lost again.

Footsteps sounded on the floorboards, and he turned to see Josephine and Lucilius enter the sitting room. Gen and Mark trailed in behind them, and they all stopped and stared at O'Neal.

"O'Neal?" Gen took a step closer, pausing a few feet from him.

"I remember you, Genesis Isherwood," he whispered softly.

Gen gasped in surprise, closed the remaining distance between them, and wrapped her arms around him.

O'Neal heard laughter and felt someone thumping him on the back as the others swarmed around him.

"I can't believe this," someone said.

O'Neal concentrated. The voice was gruff and

deep, and judging from the direction it came from, it could only have been Mark Reynolds.

Mark Reynolds, protector to Genesis Isherwood, the current nail bearer and leader of the group staying at the Triple 7 ranch.

And the Triple 7 ranch was owned by...O'Neal growled internally as he willed his concentration back to the present, fighting the flow of intrusive images.

"He looks okay," Isabella said.

Josephine waved a hand in O'Neal's face.

"You have very short hair," he commented.

"Yeah, I do," Josephine said, laughing as she rubbed her head with her hand.

"Josephine Baddock, it's good to see you," O'Neal said.

"It's good to see you too," she grinned.

O'Neal looked around the group again. Someone was missing.

"Where is Myrddin Emrys Wylit?"

"Who's that?" Josephine whispered.

"It's my granddad," Gen informed the group.

"How does he know our full names? And why is he saying it that way?" Isabella asked, also whispering.

O'Neal resisted the urge to tilt his head to the side as he looked at Isabella. "I am right here," he said loudly.

"My granddad has gone travelling," Gen explained. "He said he needed to check out a lead. It's good to see you're okay, O'Neal."

"My name is David."

"Then you must call me Gen."

O'Neal nodded. He enjoyed the warm feeling that swelled within him, and the looks of encouragement from the people around him assured him he'd done the right thing. He just had to remain focused, or he'd slip away again.

Candice was happy with the preparations she'd made to get the ball rolling. Surprise was the only way to strike a killing blow to an enemy many times stronger than oneself. And the prey she hunted was the strongest of them all. Candice wanted her victim to feel the same loss she'd had to go through. It wasn't enough to put an end to him; he had to suffer and see his loved ones suffer.

So, Candice had put her plan in motion.

Obtaining the crown of thorns was paramount. The blood of the resurrected Christ held the most potent power known in this world and beyond. Having it would give her the means to execute her strategy.

She looked at the glass case in her hands with joy, oblivious to the buildings that whisked past the window as the driver sped back to her hotel.

The young man in front of her was huge. The sleeves of his black suit seemed strained against his bulging muscles as he gripped the steering wheel.

He was one of many grunts Candice paid to protect her assets, in this case, herself. Her men were dispensable but loyal—as long as they were paid. And Candice made sure they were rewarded well for their loyalty.

She opened the glass case reverently and broke off one of the thorns. Then, she gingerly covered the case again and placed it on the seat next to her, took a vial from her pocket and dropped the thorn inside, and whispered a few words.

The words of power whirled toward the vial as they left her mouth.

Spell-crafting was part gift and part belief. She could do basic spells and even sense when magic was released because it was in her blood. But she wasn't as gifted as her enemy, who seemed to have been bathed in magic.

When her spell settled on the vial, the thorn within turned purple. She stared at it in disbelief.

The blood on the thorn was potent, but she had been played.

The crown of thorns in her possession had never touched the head of the Jewish Messiah.

"Turn the car around, Josef. We need to pay Mr. Lorenzo a visit."

Anger rose within her as the limousine made a U-turn. She clenched the vial tightly and felt a biting pain as it shattered, the glass pieces piercing her closed palm. Candice ignored the pain.

She had an account to settle with Lorenzo Auction House.

Lorenzo Lamas was born Michael Pike. At an early age, he realized the name 'Pike' would get him nowhere. 'Michael' would have been okay if he wanted to become a counsellor or a priest, but Lorenzo had no intention of taking the straight and narrow, not after the hunger he'd seen and experienced. The starving populations of the slums of Naples didn't go by names like Peter or Charles.

When he was eight years old, Lorenzo had stood in the rain and watched a small television set through the glass pane. A movie was playing, and though he hadn't seen most of it, he was enthralled by the main star: a handsome, well-built, no-nonsense type.

He waited in the rain for the end credits and was amazed to read that the lead character was called Lorenzo Lamas.

That night was the start of Lorenzo's rise from the gutters of Naples. Now, he was a supplier. His business dealt with many things, mundane and exotic. He could find anything and deliver any pleasure known to man.

Lorenzo built an empire through blood and sweat; some of it his, but most from bodies that now littered the bottom of the Sarno River.

He poured himself a glass of Barolo wine and sipped it as he walked to the chair in his study.

It had been a good day; the auction went even better than he'd hoped. Who knew people would go so wild for antiquities?

The leather seat squeaked as he sank his bulky

weight into it, and he sighed contentedly and closed his eyes.

Then, from a corner of his study, someone cleared their throat.

Lorenzo grew ice cold and bolted upright to peer into the darkness.

"Who's there? Show yourself before you become a lifeless husk."

Lorenzo tried to calm the rapid beating of his heart. His doctor had warned him to take things easy after he'd suffered a mild heart attack a few months earlier. He wasn't in his prime anymore, and being overweight wasn't helping his health. But that didn't mean he had to show fear in the face of his adversaries.

"Who are you?" he demanded.

"I have one question. Did you know the crown of thorns was a fake?"

The voice was soft-spoken and mature. Lorenzo guessed the speaker was a middle-aged man. Alarm bells were going off in his mind. Every instinct was telling him that the intruder was dangerous.

Lorenzo leaned forward and set his glass of wine down on the solid mahogany desk, his other hand reaching underneath it to press the silent-alarm button.

"I don't know who you are or how you got in here, but you've made the biggest mistake of your life," he said.

His men would storm the study in the next two minutes. He vowed to use the time to find out who the stranger worked for, then use him to send them a message.

No one messed with Lorenzo Lamas.

The stranger emerged from the shadows and approached the desk. He had neatly-combed, white hair and walked with quiet confidence, adjusting the cuffs of his black tuxedo.

When the man smiled, Lorenzo felt like a mouse in the paw of a tiger.

Suddenly, the door to the study burst open and three bodyguards stormed in. As they aimed their FN P90s at the stranger, Lorenzo got to his feet.

"You dare to come to my house and threaten me. Who sent you?"

The stranger still had a smile plastered on his face.

What kind of a person smiles when three machine guns are pointed at their face?

"Answer my question, Mr. Lorenzo, and I will leave," the man said, as calm and collected as ever. "Are you aware that the crown of thorns you auctioned tonight was a fake?"

"What are you talking about?" Lorenzo snapped. "I ask the questions here. Who sent you? You can make it easy on yourself by answering my question, or we can do this the hard way."

Who the heck was this man?

"It seems you don't know anything after all," the man intoned.

Lorenzo had had enough. No one came to his house and mouthed off like this.

"Kill the fool," Lorenzo spat. Maybe the man's dead body would provide the answers he needed.

The guards raised their guns, and Lorenzo heard the stranger whisper something.

His eyes widened in disbelief as he saw his bodyguards struggling to pull their triggers. "What is going on? Kill him!"

Lorenzo realized he was shaking. The guards started screaming; their guns were glowing red in their hands. When they tried to let go, the weapons hovered in mid-air for a few seconds before clattering to the floor.

"What in the bloody hell is going on?"

"That should be my line, don't you think?" a petite blonde said, walking into the study.

Candice quickly sized up the situation in the study and knew that she should be worried. The elderly man had a disarming smile that made the hair on her arms tingle in alarm.

The man knew magic, and that was enough to make her anxious. So, she did what she always did when she was concerned.

Candice channelled as much fire magic as she could summon and blasted it at the elderly man. The flames engulfed him. He screamed as he burned and ran out of the study, the bodyguards scrambling out of his way.

She dusted off her hands, and Lorenzo swallowed audibly.

"That was disappointing."

Candice was surprised that she'd read the elderly man wrong, but she was relieved by the outcome. She had recognized him from the auction when she first entered the study; he was the one who had cast the spell while everyone was bidding for the crown of thorns.

She hadn't been able to determine the nature of the spell but had detected it, nonetheless.

Which reminded her...

"Do you know you sold me a fake, Mr. Lorenzo?" She smiled cheerfully at the auction dealer, though she was still seething on the inside. Lorenzo glanced at his hoodlums for help, and Candice turned to them.

"I have things to discuss with your boss, boys." She snapped her fingers and a tongue of fire licked from her hand. Though they were brutes, the guards understood the law of the jungle. They knew when they were in the presence of a greater predator. They scrambled over each other to be the first to escape the study, and within seconds, Candice was alone with Lorenzo.

"Now, where were we?" she said as she sat down on the edge of his desk.

The fat man slumped down into his chair, and she knew she was staring at a broken person.

"Please, don't kill me. I acquired that piece from the curator, the curator of the National Museum. She said she found it in storage."

Candice tapped her lip with her finger as she deliberated her next course of action.

"I am telling you the truth; I swear on my mother's grave."

"Silence." She flicked her hand, and a band of air wrapped around Lorenzo's throat. He wheezed and choked as Candice left the study.

Myrddin had sensed the blonde woman's presence moments before she interrupted his questioning, which gave him enough time to create an invisible shield that covered his suit.

When she shot the fireball at him, he almost deflected it back at her but instead chose to be creative and do something no one would expect.

He allowed the fire to wrap around his body as he ran out of the room, quickly casting a listening spell. Once outside the study, he killed the flames and hurried out of the compound toward where his rental car was parked. He got into the front seat and activated the second part of the spell. He listened in as the blonde woman questioned the auction dealer.

The National Museum of Castel Sant'Angelo was in Rome. It would take more than two hours to get there.

Myrddin turned the ignition and navigated the car back into the flow of traffic to head out of town. He had hoped to be done with antiquities, but if the genuine crown of thorns still existed, he needed to secure it before someone else did.

4

Garth Armstrong scratched his week-old beard as he tried to make sense of the pyramid of photos he had taped all over the walls of his rundown motel room.

Standing a few inches over six feet, Garth was tall and slim, or—as his instructor used to say when he was in a good mood—lean like a coyote.

He hated that description, but despite how hard he tried, he never filled out and became brawny like his peers.

He caught a glimpse of himself in the mirror on the dressing table and grimaced at his unkempt hair and beard. Personal hygiene had been the least of his worries for some time now. What use was shaving in the face of the approaching apocalypse? Would he be a better fighter if he had a good haircut?

Maybe he could cut down his enemies with his razor-sharp jawline? Not that his jaw had ever been very angular. He turned his attention back to the pictures against the wall.

At the top of the pyramid was a photograph of Lucilius, and beneath that were three photos showing three individuals Garth had identified as Genesis Isherwood, Mark Reynolds, and Melvin Gourdeau. Beneath those were three more people, but he hadn't been able to identify them yet.

He had been after Lucilius ever since he'd heard that one of the four horsemen of the apocalypse had surfaced in Europe. Until recently, he had been on a wild goose chase, pursuing false trails and loose ends.

Then an informant sent a report to the Citadel of an abnormal spike in spiritual energy. Headquarters deemed the information unimportant and ignored the report, but not Garth. He knew the source of the intel. The informant in question was a spiritual bloodhound, able to detect even the minutest spike in magical essence from a mile away. If he detected an anomaly, it needed to be taken seriously. So, Garth followed the lead to Canada.

Who would have thought that one of the four horsemen would show up in a backwater town like Dundurn?

Garth still had no idea what had caused the spike in the spiritual ether, but he was grateful for the informant's work. If everything went well, he would go down in history as the only human to have captured one of the horsemen.

His phone vibrated in his pants pocket, interrupting his thoughts. He dug it out with a scowl and looked at the number as he tapped the answer button.

"What?" he snapped.

Garth didn't take his eyes off the photos on the wall as he listened to the caller on the other end of the line.

"I'm busy right now," he said, hanging up and sighing.

The caller was someone he couldn't ignore. He gave the wall of pictures one final look as he picked up his jacket and left the motel room.

The crescent moon shed just enough light for Garth to survey the deserted playground. Always extra careful, Garth arrived half an hour earlier than the agreed time and waited behind a tall shrub. Everything seemed in order; there were no hidden Citadel agents lying in wait to grab him.

Under normal circumstances, he would have taken the opportunity to stroll around the park, pondering life and his place in the greater scheme of things.

He considered doing just that for a moment, but his introspection was interrupted when a car parked at the playground's entrance. Moments later, two men in black suits got out.

Garth recognized one of the men, but he couldn't place the younger of the two.

The older man was William O'Toole, an agent with jet-black hair, a friendly face, and a lean but muscular build. The younger man seemed to be in his early twenties. He had a bulkier physique that didn't match his company suit and tie.

Who still wears ties on assignment?

The getup made the younger man look like a college kid sitting for his first job interview.

Garth emerged from his hiding spot and gave the two men a brisk wave.

"Hello, William,"

"Good evening, Garth." William was an easy-going guy most of the time, but Garth knew he was a stickler for the rules.

"Who's the kid?" he asked, sighing internally.

"This is Braddock Hangers. Graduated top of his class," William informed him.

"What? Graduated from high school? When did HQ start picking them so young?" Braddock clenched his fists in anger.

"Hey, why don't you tell boy scout here to dial it down a notch," Garth said. Braddock took a step toward Garth, but William held him back with a raised arm.

Garth raised an eyebrow at William, who shrugged. The expression on his face seemed to say that he didn't have anything to do with Braddock's attitude.

"The Chairman sent him. You need to come back with us, Garth," William explained.

"Can't do that."

"You need to come back, Garth. This assignment wasn't sanctioned by any of the instructors or management."

"You don't know the gravity of this thing, William," Garth protested. "One of the horsemen is in a town nearby. One of the horsemen!"

William shook his head dismissively. "Come back and file a report. You know there's a chain of command. Heck, you could have been an instructor, Garth."

Garth gritted his teeth at William's jab. Yeah, he could have been an instructor if he had played along with the Citadel's politics. But he couldn't just stand by while innocent lives were in danger.

The Citadel prided itself on being the watchman and the last bulwark against evil, but now, with real danger looming, its leadership sat back and did nothing.

No one took the informant's report seriously.

"I can't come back, William. I need to see this through."

"Disregarding authority only leads to chaos," William said.

"Spoken like a true sycophant. I've heard that line countless times. We have a chance here, William. We shouldn't be arguing. Join me. I could use your skills." Having William on his side would be a huge plus and would greatly increase their chances of victory over Lucilius.

"Sorry, Garth. I'll say it again. Come back with us. I'll make sure I carry your report to the Chairman's desk myself."

"And if I refuse?"

Garth saw William nod in Braddock's direction.

"That's where he comes him. I've seen the kid fight, Garth. He was taught by the best."

"I bet."

"Look, let's not turn this into a sordid affair, okay? Don't let your pride get in the way of common sense. You can't do this alone. You just admitted that you need my help. If you're right, I don't think the horseman's going anywhere soon."

"You don't know that for certain, William. I'm seeing this through."

"Is that your final answer?"

Garth locked eyes with William and refused to look away. He believed the course he was on was the right one, and he wouldn't back down for anyone.

Braddock took a knuckle duster from his pocket and secured it on his right hand.

"Really, William?" he scoffed.

William shrugged again, and Garth turned his attention to Braddock.

A knuckle duster was a nasty piece of work. Not only was it a hardened piece of iron that could break bones and crack skulls, but it also acted as a channel for the wearer's magic.

Garth studied Braddock's body language as the young man advanced, then raised a hand to implore him to stop. Confused, Braddock turned to William for guidance. William nodded, and Braddock took a step back.

"What do they teach you youngsters nowadays?" Garth asked with a sneer and a shake of his head. He saw William frown and smirked at him.

William must have thought Garth was giving up or something. Garth was very happy to disappoint him.

"Magic combat 101: always create a containment spell. That way, you're sure of two things. One, whatever happens within the containment area will stay there. Two, no one outside the containment area can get hurt or even be aware of what's happening inside it. I thought you said this guy was at the top of his class?"

"Stop trying to delay the inevitable," Braddock said, speaking up for the first time.

"Ah, the star pupil speaks! The Citadel's standards must be trash now. Back in my days, you'd be relegated to a cook; that's if you have the IQ for that."

Braddock rushed at him in anger, the knuckle dusters sparkling with static electricity as he swung.

Garth had been an average pupil at the Citadel; his magic was never exceptional. His elemental spells were okay, a little above the intermediate level, but there were other kids whose spells carried way more punch.

There was one area, however, in which Garth shone like a prodigy—spell crafting.

The shields he crafted through his spells had given him a reputation that was on par with that of their top instructors. His shields were a marvel to behold, just like the one he had created around his body this night.

Braddock's fist landed, and the air in front of Garth exploded in a shower of flickering blue sparks as his shield held, and Braddock stumbled back from the backlash of his strike.

Garth quickly rotated his right hand in wide concentric circles to create a containment shield around the playground. It was late, so he didn't expect to see any passersby, but he would feel bad if someone got hurt, and it was better to be safe.

The spell took only a fraction of a second and, as Braddock prepared to attack again, Garth strengthened the shield around his body. Just in time, too, as an unseen force suddenly slammed into it. Garth grunted in pain.

He recognized William's magic. He was an air user, and Garth had seen the magician stop bullets with only the force of his magic.

William rose into the air and prepared his spell for another shot. Meanwhile, Braddock stepped closer to Garth's shield to make another attempt at shattering it.

Garth knew it would take William a couple of seconds to prepare, so he momentarily released the shield over his body and turned sideways as Braddock swung. The punch went wide, leaving Braddock's left side exposed.

Garth learned a bitter lesson while at the Citadel Training Institute. Like every magic user, he'd been dependent on magic and had often been bested by people who were experts at unarmed combat, even when they had no powers. As a result, he made it his mission to learn other forms of fighting to augment his magical ability, and he used that knowledge with devasting results.

Garth created a small shield around his fist and drove it into Braddock's exposed ribs. It connected like a sledgehammer, and Garth heard the sound of a rib cracking. The force of the strike lifted Braddock of his feet, tempting Garth to take advantage of the gap and throw another punch, but he knew that would be a mistake. He turned his attention back to William.

The air crackled as William completed his spell and lightning gathered around him. Garth barely got his shield in place before a bolt struck, shattering it on impact. The force of the strike threw him backward. He tumbled onto the soft sand but quickly turned it into a roll, his hands moving in circles to create three new shields around him.

Another bolt of lightning shattered the outer shield.

How many more of those can William manage? he thought as the second shield exploded in blue fragments.

Sure enough, William descended gracefully back to the ground to take a breath.

Throwing high-energy spells was very taxing, and Garth knew William would need to recycle his essence before he could do anything as dangerous as lightning bolts again.

Not that Garth would give him the opportunity.

That was another beautiful thing about his ability: creating shields didn't cost him much energy. And, while he would eventually get tired, he still had enough juice left to put William and his young partner to sleep.

He turned back to face Braddock, who was busy gathering a spell in his outstretched hands.

What the...

"Is he crazy?" Garth screamed at William.

Braddock's spell had created a tiny maelstrom, and Garth felt particles of sand pierce his cheeks and arm. He stared in amazement as a void vortex appeared between Braddock's hands.

Garth swore. William hadn't been joking; the kid had talent. It was almost impossible to create void energy; it was the antithesis of most spells. They were unstable and needed spiritual strength and stamina to maintain.

The void energy sizzled as the vortex wobbled and expanded to the size of a golf ball.

"Release the spell, kid. You can't maintain it," Garth shouted. "You'll get yourself killed." The whine of the strong wind scattered his warning. His eyes widened as the void energy changed shape, pulsing and writhing in Braddock's hands as it grew larger and larger. William looked around for shelter, but Garth knew that nowhere within a fifty-foot radius would be safe.

He swore to himself again and prepared a shield, working fast against the raging wind and smarting sand. The shield had a bluish tint—a result of the amount of essence he'd poured into it. Garth then created three more shields around himself, William, and Braddock. No sooner had the last shield snapped into place than the ball of wobbling void energy exploded.

The shield around Braddock's hands cracked

with a resounding bang. He and William were blown aside, their shields obliterated by the blast. The energy washed over the playground.

Garth fell to his knees as the void energy hit his shield. He continued pouring essence into his shield as it cracked, racing to restore the damage, again and again. Around him, the void energy washed over the playground. The merry-go-round was spinning out of control, the swings flapping around wildly, threatening to break free from the metal structure that held them in place.

Garth was running out of essence; he didn't have long. He shouted as his shield finally shattered, and he was blown backward onto the grass. Just like that, the wind was gone.

Groaning, Garth got to his feet.

Somehow, William had survived. He was sitting in the sandpit, trying to catch his breath. Garth gave him a glance as he hurried toward Braddock, who was struggling to his feet.

Garth didn't have any essence left to create a shield, but he drove his fist into the young man's face. Braddock fell on his back, and Garth drove his foot into his stomach.

"What the bloody hell was that?" Garth shouted as he kicked the now-defenceless kid, who could only groan in pain.

"Stop, Garth, before you kill him."

He pushed aside his raging anger and turned to William, who seemed to be cradling a broken arm. His once pristine suit was shredded and dirty.

"I'll go after this horseman," Garth said. "Maybe, with his death, the prophesied apocalypse can be avoided."

"Let the Citadel help, Garth. You can't do this on your own. You know what they do to those that go rogue."

"Then tell them. I'll need all the help I can get. They need to see the gravity of the situation. The horseman can disappear anytime. I can't wait for the Citadel to call a conclave meeting. You know it will take too long."

"That is the Citadel's way, Garth. It has and will always be. Who are we to try and change things? They will come down on you hard for your disobedience. Let me take you back, and let's resolve this peacefully."

Garth considered William's offer for a second, then shook his head.

"I know you mean well, William, but I'm willing to pay the price to see this through. For the sake of humanity, I'll lay down my life."

Garth limped toward the edge of the playground. He was completely defenceless, drained of essence, but he could see that William and Braddock weren't any better off. He stopped and turned back.

"Let them know, William, if they come for me, they should be prepared. I won't surrender easily. I know their tricks, and I will do what it takes to fulfill this assignment. Nothing will stand in my way."

With that, Garth turned around and limped away from the playground.

5

"We have a problem," Isabella said, rushing into the living room.

Gen closed her laptop and set it down on the coffee table. Isabella joined her on the sofa and placed a tablet in her lap.

Gen stared at the screen in confusion.

"What am I looking at?"

Isabella reached over Gen's shoulder and clicked play on the YouTube video clip.

It was grainy, but Gen could identify Ava and her mother, Derby. The video showed Gen healing Ava's broken ankle.

She remembered the incident like it was yesterday. She'd gone to town to see Theo and had spotted little Ava limping painfully. Moved by Ava's infirmity, Gen reached out to heal her.

"What's wrong?" Gen asked Isabella. Although she didn't like the fact that someone had recorded the healing, there wasn't anything she could do about it.

"Keep watching," Isabella said.

A face appeared on the screen, a lanky man in his early thirties. His eyes flashed angrily as he ranted at the camera.

"We have to put a stop to swindlers and fakes. This woman, this Genesis Isherwood, took advantage of a poor woman and her kid for her own personal gain. People like her have to be stopped. Enough is enough."

Gen looked at Isabella in shock. What was going on?

"Who's this?" she asked.

"His name is Russell Patel. He has a small following, but he's never been this vocal about anybody or any issue. I don't understand what his problem is, but he seems to have singled you out."

Gen sighed as she handed the tablet back to Isabella.

"Should I be worried?"

"I don't know. People are listening to him, and it looks like he's riling them up. Some of the comments are pretty bad."

"So, what do we do?" Gen asked with another sigh. This was the last thing they needed.

Isabella shrugged and tucked the tablet underneath her armpit.

"We could come up with our own video, explaining our side of the story."

Gen liked the fact that Isabella included herself

in the proposed solution. She had been wary about having a reporter amongst the group, but Isabella had proven her loyalty over time. She'd convinced Gen to create a YouTube channel, and they'd been uploading the occasional video. To Gen's surprise, the channel had been gathering a following, although she still didn't really get how just talking about life could help anyone. Isabella assured her that there were people waiting to hear what she had to say.

"I don't know if releasing our own video would help," Gen mused. "Wouldn't that just make it look like we have something to hide if we acknowledge this...Russell guy?"

"True," Isabella said with a rueful smile. "But, that said, I think we have to look into him; find out what his story is. I'll head over to town and catch up with Theo. Maybe he can get us something."

Gen watched Isabella leave the sitting room and picked up her laptop again. She tried to concentrate on the baking video she had been watching earlier, but her mind kept wandering back to the angry YouTuber.

She closed the video and signed into her email account. There were only messages from her bank and newsletters she'd subscribed to over the years. She was about to log out when she saw an email notification from a sender she recognized.

Benedict Callaway.

She hadn't thought of him in a long time. She knew Benedict at university—he had graduated a few years ahead of her.

Gen opened the email and glanced through it curiously. It didn't say much. Basically, Benedict was just letting her know that he was sending her a parcel.

How strange, she thought. They hadn't been very close. What could he possibly be sending her? And why now?

Patrick Anderson believed that a job was a job. Some were good, and some were crap, but he gave his all to everything he and his team were hired to do.

Patrick had protected presidents and captured tyrants. Unfortunately, he'd also killed people that needed killing. He didn't like it, but a job was a job.

Maybe that was why his mouth felt full of ash as he glanced around the small sitting room that had once belonged to a man called Benedict Callaway. Benedict had annoyed some very powerful people, and Patrick had been called in to handle the situation.

A job was a job.

Patrick cradled the FN SCAR assault rifle in his arms as his men rummaged through the apartment. He was wearing a black special-ops tactical uniform but without headgear. The warpaint on his face blended into the dark ambience of the room. His team wore similar outfits, but their heads and faces were shrouded in black head gear that left only their eyes exposed.

"We've swept the house. He was telling the truth," one of them informed him.

Patrick nodded and headed for the door, taking out a satellite phone and dialling a number as he stepped over Benedict Callaway's dead body. Patrick cleared his throat as the call connected. He could hear his employer's faint breathing on the other end of the line.

"Doctor Benedict made a copy of his work and sent it to a friend," Patrick said quietly.

"You are sure he made only one copy?" the voice asked.

When Patrick first went freelance, he made a game of guessing the nationality of his employers from their voices. This accent sounded Asian, perhaps Indian or Pakistani.

"The only copy he made was the one he sent." Patrick was sure of this. His team's search was thorough.

"And you know where?"

"Yes. Dundurn, Canada."

"Amber Corporation needs that drive. We can't afford for it to get into the hands of our competition."

"I understand," Patrick tried to reassure the voice.

"Do what you must."

The line went dead. Patrick folded away the antenna of the satellite phone and returned it to his pocket.

"Wrap it up, guys. We have another assignment," he said.

Patrick didn't like hurting women, but a job was a job. His clients relied on him to get things done because he always delivered. He wasn't ready to change that pattern for anybody.

Myrddin was walking along the Sant'Angelo bridge toward the Mausoleum of Hadrian, or the National Museum of Castel Sant'Angelo, as it was now called. Memories of previous visits flooded his mind as he admired the statues of the angels that adorned the guardrails to either side of the bridge. He smiled as he imagined how the crowd of tourists around him would react if they knew he had a hand in building the museum.

Myrddin shook his head and hurried to the museum. He didn't have time to dally. He suspected that the blonde woman from the auction house would soon make an appearance, and he needed information before that happened.

He weaved his way through the throng of admiring people and made his way to the courtyard, spotting the curator immediately. She was dressed in a cream blouse and white pants, and she seemed to be in her mid-forties. She had an engaging smile, which Myrddin returned.

"Eh, Mr. Gourdeau?" she ventured.

"Yes."

Myrddin shook the hand she offered and followed the curator to the side of the courtyard. They were surrounded by tourists, which made the meeting safe for both parties.

"You said you were interested in donating a historical item to the museum?" the curator asked, getting straight to business.

Myrddin saw the curiosity in the woman's eyes, but he could tell she was also guarded and distrustful.

"Yes, I do. I was referred to you by Lorenzo Lamas." Myrddin watched the curator closely as he spoke the name. She appeared ignorant, betraying almost no reaction, but he had lived too long not to spot the flash of recognition that flitted through the woman's eyes.

"I am sorry, but the name doesn't ring a bell," she said. "The museum deals with a lot of patrons and benefactors. If you can show me the item you brought..."

Myrddin dug into his pocket and brought out the foot nail. He watched the curator's eyes widen in amazement as she stretched out a quivering hand toward the nail.

"Is that...?"

Myrddin nodded, and the curator gasped. He felt a twinge of guilt at the deception; he had bought an ordinary nail from a hardware shop. A simple illusion spell made it look aged and weathered, and he had siphoned a little power into the nail so it would throb with essence—just enough to make someone see what they wanted to see.

The curator saw an aged relic that had a semblance of power, and her mind came to the only logical conclusion. She believed that Myrddin was holding one of the three nails of power.

"Like I said, Lorenzo Lamas gave me your number."

The curator's hand was still shaking as it lingered near the nail.

"You want to keep this here?" she asked him reverently.

"I am considering it. I only have a couple of questions."

At that, the curator looked up, and their eyes met.

"You sold Lorenzo an item. The crown of thorns. Where is the original?"

The curator's eyes flicked back to the nail, and she licked her lips.

"I don't know what you're talking about."

He clenched his fist and cut of the flow of power to the nail in his hand.

"Then I guess we're done here." He turned around and started walking back toward the exit.

"Wait!" she called, right on cue.

He stopped and turned around, waiting as the curator walked toward him.

"I didn't know the crown was a fake. One of our patrons donated it. Said he found it in his attic. The artifact looked real enough to me."

"So, you decided to sell it."

If Myrddin had hoped to make the curator guilty, he failed, as she merely shrugged in agreement.

"The museum didn't know of the crown," she said. "No harm was done, and it will probably end up somewhere safer than this museum."

Myrddin grunted in annoyance. He disliked the fact that, for some people, the end justified the means.

"Who gave you the crown?"

The curator hesitated. "I get the nail in exchange?"

"Yes."

She seemed to make up her mind. "His name is Marco Brambilla. He has a villa at the edge of town. A very private man, if you know what I mean."

Myrddin understood perfectly.

He brought out the nail and placed it in the curator's shaking hands. He could feel the waves of greed pouring out of her, and he pitied her.

"If you sell this, my advice would be for you to skip town—for good."

Without waiting for her answer, Myrddin turned and walked away, sensing the curator scuttle from the courtyard behind him.

Patrick dangled his hand from the window of the black sedan as they sped down the highway. He watched the landscape race past as Carter, a burly man in his late thirties and Patrick's second-in-command, drove them to Dundurn.

The scientist, Doctor Benedict, had admitted to sending the memory card to an old schoolmate.

They were on the way there now and, by sunset, he would have the card in his hands.

A job is a job.

He tried not to dwell on what he might need to do to get it back, instead closing his eyes to enjoy the cool breeze blowing through his hair.

6

ark tried not to let his concern show as he drove the van into town, but he could see from the frown on Gen's face that she wasn't fooled. She was fully aware of the gravity of the situation. Mark watched the YouTube video, and he knew from experience that people could turn violent if they thought they were fighting for the right thing.

The drive was quiet, even with five of them in the van. Isabella and Lucilius were sitting in the back with O'Neal, who had surprised everyone by asking to come along. Gen was sitting in the passenger seat next to Mark. This meant only Josephine was back at the Triple 7 ranch to keep an eye on things.

"Have you heard from Myrddin?" Mark glanced at Gen.

"He called last night. He said he was going to take a couple more days to look into a crown," Gen answered.

"A crown?"

She nodded, and Mark left it at that. Gen hadn't told him exactly why Myrddin had left for Europe, and Mark didn't see any reason to pry. No need for him to worry about the strongest magician in the world.

"Who's after a crown?" Isabella asked from the back.

"It seems Myrddin has a taste for royalty," Mark joked. Not that he'd blame Gen's grandfather if he decided to overthrow a kingdom. Heck, who would be able to stop him?

He listened as Gen repeated what she'd told him to Isabella, studying O'Neal in the rearview mirror. Their eyes met and Mark smiled, glad that O'Neal's resurgence hadn't been only temporary. The doctor still didn't say much, but Mark was okay with that. He no longer had that lost, faraway look that plagued him after he was given his abilities. Although Mark still didn't fully understand his explanation of what had happened, O'Neal was now a fully functioning member of the group.

Once they arrived in town, Mark headed for the sheriff's office and parked right outside the building. The group piled out of the van and headed toward the entrance with Gen in the lead. Only Mark and Lucilius hung back, both of them eyeing the environment discreetly.

The person they'd come to see was lounging on a porch chair in front of the sheriff's office with his legs stretched out before him.

Mark studied Theo Cuttaham, the acting sheriff of the little town of Dundurn. His initial impression of Theo had been that he was a kid trying to fill his daddy's boots and failing miserably. But his opinion had changed since then, and he now knew that Theo's disarming, boyish looks belied his intelligence.

Leaning against the van, Mark watched as Gen embraced the acting sheriff, who had scrambled to his feet when he spotted her approaching. He didn't detect any suspicious behaviour or intent as he sized him up. He knew Theo was on their side, but Mark was Gen's protector. It was his job to be paranoid and suspicious of everyone. He turned his attention back to scanning the vicinity, noting the few elderly residents trailing up the sidewalk and peering out from behind their curtains.

Dundurn was a small town, and anyone visiting the sheriff's office was bound to draw attention. The fact that Gen had come with strangers only compounded the situation. Some residents knew Mark, but this would be the first time they'd get a glimpse of O'Neal, Isabella, and Lucilius.

The former immortal still hung back from the chatting group, choosing to keep watch with his sparring partner. Mark knew Lucilius was just as conscious of his environment as himself. The man looked completely relaxed, but he knew he was ready to spring into action at the slightest sign of trouble. Mark wouldn't admit it, but he felt better knowing Lucilius was around. A certain bond had formed between Lucilius and Gen—a bond that Mark knew he didn't need to worry about. Lucilius took Gen's safety as seriously as Mark did—maybe even more so—seeing as Gen had played such an important role in converting the former accursed to their side.

Mark felt at ease as he watched Lucilius scan the area for danger.

Two sets of eyes were better than one.

Carter made his way back to the car that was parked some miles away from the Triple 7 ranch, where intel had placed the target. Patrick felt a recon mission was required to gather more information, so he booked two rooms in a motel on the outskirts of the nearest town and took Carter along to look around the target property.

"The ranch is empty, but it's the right place," Carter reported as he opened the front car door on the passenger side and got in.

"Did you find the wristwatch?" Patrick asked. The scientist told them he had put the memory card in his watch and mailed it to their target.

Carter shook his head, and Patrick grimaced. It would all have been so tidy and simple if they had just found it. There wouldn't be any need to hurt anybody. But now, he'd need to extract all the information he could from the target. He would need to find out whether she had discovered the memory card and its contents and if she had told anybody else. Regardless of the answer, the target's life was forfeited.

A job was a job.

They drove back to the ranch in comfortable silence. Theo had agreed to help, and Mark knew the young sheriff would go out of his way to supply Gen with the assistance she requested. Theo had grown up with Gen and had a secret crush on her. Well, not so secret, since Mark had seen it the first time he'd laid eyes on the kid.

Gen assured Mark that she didn't reciprocate Theo's feelings and, though Mark liked to think he wasn't the jealous type, he was very glad to hear this.

He hadn't come to Dundurn with the intention of falling for the nail bearer, but things played out differently. His feelings for Gen had grown from a mere assignment to wanting to be with her all the time.

As he turned off the main road toward the Triple 7 ranch, he saw a car approaching from the other direction. There weren't any other properties on this road, and while there was any number of possible reasons for a car to be here, Mark felt tension creep into his bones. He slowed the van down to a cruise and slowly passed the silver Hyundai Elantra, glancing at the two men who sat in the front. They had the hardened look of outsiders, and Mark spotted a tattoo on the wrist of the man in the passenger seat.

He felt his blood freeze as he recognized the tattoo, resisting the urge to look back as the car turned onto the main road and drove off. Mark looked up into the rearview mirror and found Lucilius staring at him.

Trouble had come to Dundurn.

Patrick couldn't believe his luck.

For a moment, he'd locked eyes with the target. She looked exactly like the photo in the file.

Genesis Isherwood.

He was about to tell Carter to turn around when he spotted the driver of the van. The man had tried to look disinterested, but Patrick had seen the glance he had thrown their way.

The driver was a professional, and Patrick had counted at least two other people in the back seat. If they were also pros like the driver, he was uncertain about the odds of accomplishing his mission.

He kept quiet as the vehicles passed each other, and Carter rejoined the main road.

They'd need to come back. Next time, with the whole team.

Mark brought the van to a halt and opened his door to get out. He heard the back door open and footsteps follow him as he ran to the arch at the entrance of the Triple 7 ranch. There was no sign of the Hyundai.

"Trouble," Lucilius said quietly as he stopped at Mark's side. It was more of a statement than a question, but Mark nodded in agreement.

It seemed Gen's feeling of unease was warranted.

"We'll have to keep watch going forward. Those two will definitely be back, and we have to be ready when they do," Mark said.

"Why wait? Why don't we hunt them down and put them out of their misery?" Lucilius asked flatly. Mark glanced at the former accursed. Although he agreed with that approach, he knew Gen never would. And his job was to protect the nail bearer.

She glanced between Mark and Lucilius, her brow creased with concern.

"What's going on?" Gen asked, her brow creased with concern.

One of the qualities Mark found so endearing about Gen was her ability to immediately understand a situation and work with it. She waited for him to answer and folded her arms across her chest.

"You were right. I believe trouble is coming," Mark said.

"The silver car?"

He raised an eyebrow at her question.

"Yes. I didn't think you noticed."

"The nail bearer is a warrior and shouldn't be looked down on," Lucilius said.

"I agree," Mark concurred.

"I've been around you for a while now, Mark," she said. "I know how you think. I thought you were going to leap out of the van and pounce on that car. What are we dealing with?"

"Can't be sure, but I think that was a reconnaissance team. They came to check out the area."

"You're sure? They couldn't be tourists that missed their way?" Gen suggested.

"No." Mark shook his head. "And they're special forces. Or ex-special forces. I saw the tattoo on one of them."

Gen didn't argue—another thing Mark loved about her. Although she could be stubborn when she wanted to, she was very practical when needed.

"Lucilius suggested we nip this in the bud," Mark added.

"You want to attack these men based on an assumption?" Gen glared at Mark and Lucilius in turn. Mark saw Lucilius fidget uncomfortably. The situation was almost comical. Lucilius was over a thousand years old and had fought in more wars than anyone Mark knew, yet he felt intimidated by Gen. She turned her stare back to Mark, but he wasn't fazed. His job was to keep her alive, even when she didn't like how he did it.

"It's not an assumption. They were here to scout the area, and they will be back. Besides, it's not like we're going to kill them."

"We will merely extract information," Lucilius added.

"By torturing them?" Gen fired back.

Lucilius remained quiet as Gen rubbed the bridge of her nose, considering their options.

"We can prepare for an attack, but no torturing anybody," Gen finally said. "You should know better, Mark."

He smiled, and Gen realized he'd been pulling her strings.

"Seriously, you've been uneasy for some time, Gen. This could be it."

Mark heard a vehicle approaching and turned around to face the road. He reached out with his essence and touched two individuals, one familiar to him. He relaxed and saw the tension on Gen's face fall away too.

"It's Josephine," he said. "She doesn't seem agitated, so I guess she's okay."

They waited as the rental car came to a stop, and Josephine emerged with some shopping bags. Lucilius rushed over to help her, and she flashed him a smile. Mark turned back to Gen, who was smiling at him knowingly.

"What?" he asked.

"You know, for someone who can sense things, you can be quite slow at times."

Mark frowned. What was she saying?

He looked back at Lucilius and noticed how his posture had relaxed. Although he didn't return Josephine's smile, Mark could see that Lucilius was comfortable in her presence.

"Could they—"

Gen cut him short with a whistle and started walking toward the house. Mark grinned and followed close behind, allowing Josephine and Lucilius some privacy.

Myrddin watched the Brambilla villa from a safe distance. He could detect the presence of countless souls he could only assume were bodyguards or security personnel. The place was a fortress, and it was guarded like one too. Whoever this Marco Brambilla was, he had paid a lot for security, and that could only mean one thing—he had something to hide.

Myrddin looked down at his clothes and wondered if they would do. He had to get to Marco Brambilla, ideally without causing a scene.

He could create an invisibility spell, but that was taxing, and he didn't know how long he'd need to remain hidden. The villa was vast and might take a while to search, so Myrddin wasn't sure he could maintain an invisibility spell for long enough, certainly not without a totem or catalyst to boost his spell.

Weighing his options, he was about to give the invisibility spell a try when he noticed another presence and heard the sound of dogs barking.

So much for that plan. There was no way he would be able to go by undetected with the dogs there to sniff him out.

One thing Myrddin was sure of was that Marco Brambilla was in the villa. He could sense a presence in a large room that he guessed was a study. Myrddin wouldn't have given the presence a second thought if not for the number of people protecting that room.

And the room was smack in the center of the villa. *Great.*

Myrddin considered using an air spell. That could work—with the right planning. He could leap-frog from rooftop to rooftop, and as long as he wasn't spotted, even the barking of the dogs wouldn't be enough to give him away.

The room was just like all the other countless motel rooms Patrick had stayed in during the many operations he'd been a part of.

The familiar, mechanical clicks and clacks of his men checking their equipment soothed his nerves and helped focus his mind as they prepared for their assault on the ranch.

There were at least five people to deal with: the target and four others, including at least one professional. He didn't get a good look at the driver, so they would have to hit hard and fast.

He hoped they still had the element of surprise on their side, but he couldn't shake the feeling that this assignment could go sideways.

7

Myrddin rotated his hand slowly, and the air around him stirred. Dust swirled as he lifted off and hovered a few feet above the ground. He didn't usually need motions to cast spells, but for what he had in mind, finesse was key.

He chanted as he hovered in the air, and an optical illusion settled around him. The space around him became distorted, the light bending and making the air shimmer until it looked as though he'd disappeared.

Maintaining this illusion would be easier than powering the invisibility spell, and it wouldn't be as taxing when combined with flying through the air.

Myrddin could barely see through the distorted air caused by his optical illusion, and he would need to pour a lot more essence into the spell to make the illusion one-way only. Instead, he decided to stretch out his essence to act like a radar. This meant he was now juggling three spells at once.

Any other magician would have found the feat almost impossible, but he was Myrddin Emrys Wylit, the greatest wizard to ever live. He had enough spiritual essence to spare.

He rose higher and flew across the grounds toward the villa. Arriving at the security fence surrounding the property, he saw that the main gate was protected by four guards and two dogs. The dogs started barking when Myrddin drew near, probably alerted by his scent. The guards looked around suspiciously, but they didn't look up, and Myrddin passed over their heads undetected.

The spell was draining his essence faster than he'd calculated, so he stopped on a rooftop to rest. His head began to pound as the weight of maintaining the three complex spells pressed on his soul. He sucked in a lungful of air and leaned against the ridge of the roof. Myrddin looked around and groaned as he realized the main building was still far away.

Maybe this wasn't the best plan.

Gen had demanded to join in the fight, and Mark couldn't change her mind. She was adamant that wherever he took his stand, she would be by his side. Mark loved the fact that she wanted to be with him, but he didn't want her to put herself in danger because of that.

So, he agreed with one condition: Gen had to follow his orders without hesitation. There was only room for one leader, and when it came to the safety of the people on the ranch, Mark's orders were final.

He stretched out his essence as far as he could manage. He could sense everything within a 400-meter radius; every ant, lizard, and creature of the night that stirred in the darkness around the ranch. There was no way anybody could sneak in without him knowing.

He could also sense the containment field that surrounded the ranch. It had initially resisted Mark's attempt to push past it, but he had overcome its power and had broken through.

Mark still believed that a good offence was the best defence, but Gen didn't give in. He just hoped he was wrong and had overreacted, but he didn't think he'd be that lucky.

Things had been peaceful for too long and, somehow, he felt more relaxed now that he knew what was coming. They had fought demons and the accursed; handling a special ops team should be a walk in the park.

Gen caught Mark's eye, and he shook his head to indicate that everything was still clear.

Myrddin wasn't sure if he had enough essence to make it to the next building, but he had to try. He decided to forego the optical illusion spell and just glide across the grounds. That meant he'd have to time his flight perfectly.

He willed the little essence he'd been able to gather into an air spell and took off. The headache returned within seconds, and he felt like throwing up. He knew he was suffering from essence overburn.

Who would have thought that the great Merlin, the wizard that had lived for centuries, would suffer from essence overburn? He wondered what the others would say.

Mark would probably find the situation hilarious. Lucilius would be more serious, perhaps frown with that condescending look that said, "I'm not surprised at your incompetence, Wizard."

Myrddin reached the next rooftop and realized that his headache had disappeared.

Could thinking about his family have restored his power?

Mark sensed the approach of two Ford Explorers as the vehicles left the main road and turned toward the ranch.

"They're here," he whispered.

He stood some meters away from the main house with Gen and Lucilius on either side of him. He would have preferred to create an ambush and have the element of surprise on their side, but Gen had frowned at what she called an "unfair fight." Their plan was now dependent on scaring the hell out of a strike team by showing them their powers.

"Two vehicles, two teams of four," Mark informed them.

Josephine and O'Neal had offered to help, but he had relegated them to backup. In other words, they would sit this one out. Josephine had seethed, but Mark hadn't been bothered and seeing Lucilius's approval only reinforced the decision.

He took comfort in the sword in his hand. Ever since Myrddin and the angel Baraqiel forged it, Mark felt a bond with the weapon. Lucilius suggested he name the sword, but Mark didn't indulge in such flights of fancy.

It was a weapon—albeit a powerful one, the bane of demons and other evil entities—but nothing more.

The vehicles cruised to a stop a few meters from the archway at the ranch's entrance. The strike team was probably puzzled seeing Mark, Gen, and Lucilius waiting there. Mark expected them to approach, perhaps thinking that the three of them were looking to parley.

He didn't mind that either. If there was a way for the night not to end in bloodshed, he would take it gladly.

Sure enough, the front doors of the leading Ford Explorer opened, and two men stepped out. They were clad in full combat gear and cradled FN SCAR assault rifles. They held the guns loosely as they approached, muzzles pointed at the ground.

Gen didn't understand what was happening, but she was glad when two men stepped out of the first SUV and headed toward them. She glanced at Mark, trying to read his body language. If anything was going to happen, she would be able to read it from his posture.

She didn't know how or why it worked, but she could tell when Mark was preparing for a fight. He was like an open book to her.

It must be to do with her being the nail bearer and Mark her protector, since she couldn't read anyone else like she could read him. She saw the slight release of tension in Mark's shoulders and the way he loosened his grip on his sword: they were going to allow the men approach them.

Gen didn't know how she felt about that. She believed talking to the men was way better than slugging it out, but she wasn't naïve enough to believe that every adversary would want to sit down for tea.

She felt the nail in her palm and took comfort in the divine object. She didn't know why, but recently she'd felt the impulse to keep the nail close to her at all times. It throbbed quietly with power, and Gen sensed holding it was the right course of action.

Lucilius couldn't believe that the nail bearer and her protector wanted a parley. Anything less than total domination would be seen as a sign of weakness, and he didn't think the two advancing men were here to talk.

They walked like predators, the same way the protector carried himself. People like that believed their combat skills were superior to every other being on the planet and, most of the time, they were correct. But the rest of the time, they were dead. Especially when they were unfortunate enough to face someone like Lucilius.

He stood poised and ready to spring into action. The holster on his hip carried Mark's famous Glock. The protector had been giving him lessons in the use of firearms and, while Lucilius still felt guns were for lesser beings, his present mortality meant he couldn't be choosy.

Patrick couldn't understand what he was seeing as they drove up to the ranch. They had hoped to storm the area under cover of darkness and terminate the target, but there she was, standing meters in front of him.

He spotted the driver of the van beside their target and couldn't shake the uneasy feeling that washed over him. *Who enters a gunfight with a sword?*

Patrick gripped his assault rifle tightly as they walked toward the three people waiting for them.

The two men stopped just outside the reach of Mark's sword. They still hadn't taken any aggressive action, presumably because they thought they had the upper hand. Both men looked forty-something; one was a little over six feet and had piercing grey eyes, while the other was shorter but bulkier.

"You are on private property."

Mark started the dialogue by giving the men the benefit of the doubt. Gen said he shouldn't ignore the possibility that they were simply lost, but the two men's combat attire and assault weapons quickly killed that notion. Still, Mark decided to indulge her optimism, at least initially.

"Let's cut the crap," the taller of the two men said, casually swinging his rifle to rest on his shoulder. He continued with an air of lazy confidence. "There's a contract out on the woman standing beside you. You can hand her over quietly, or things could get messy for you."

Mark studied the man who had spoken and figured he must be the leader.

"I'll give you the courtesy of a warning," he said. "Believe me when I tell you that you're outclassed and outgunned. This isn't an assignment that'll go the way you think. Get back into your car and get the hell out of here."

The leader laughed and beckoned over his shoulder for the rest of his team to approach. Another six men hurried out of their cars, all holding assault rifles. Within seconds, the situation would turn nasty. Mark could see the leader would attack without any scruples, believing he had superior numbers.

Myrddin felt rested, and though his goal was still far away, he believed he could get there without tiring. He didn't know what had happened, as he'd never experienced anything like what he just went through in his entire life—he was restored without any spell or intervention.

This was a different type of magic—magic that didn't depend on the user to cast a spell. *How is that even possible?* He cast the air spell and took off again. As an afterthought, he also cast the optical illusion spell again, as he had enough energy now and was getting close to his destination.

The closer Myrddin got to the main building at the center of the villa, the more guards he saw patrolling the ground below. He launched from rooftop to rooftop and finally touched down on the building next to the one that held Marco Brambilla.

An army of guards was stationed outside the main house. Two teams patrolled the area with dogs, communicating with walky-talkies. Myrddin was glad that he'd cast the illusion spell. Snipers were positioned at each of the four corners of the rooftop, and a patrol team moved around its perimeter.

He felt the headache coming back. He knew he had to come up with a plan, and quickly. The rooftop was out of the question, as he didn't think he'd be able to handle six highly trained operatives with his essence as drained as it was.

Myrddin noticed a balcony on the second floor of the house and considered his chances. If he timed it right, he could get there without being detected by the snipers or the rooftop patrol.

Taking a deep breath, he lifted off and floated toward the main house. As he neared the building, the dogs started barking below, and the men looked around in confusion. The snipers swept the area with their guns, seeking a target. The headache became a beating drum in Myrddin's skull. Suddenly, three men rushed out onto the balcony. They stopped at the edge and aimed their guns in Myrddin's direction. He froze mid-air, leaking essence as he waited, watching the guards with bated breath.

The spell held. Failing to see him, the men moved to the other end of the balcony, scanned the area, and finally went back into the house.

Myrddin drifted forward and gently landed on the balcony. He breathed a sigh of relief when his throbbing headache disappeared. He kept the illusion spell active as he walked toward the door, grateful that the dogs hadn't been brought up to the balcony, as that would have significantly complicated matters. For once, things were going according to plan. He got to the door without further incident and stretched out his senses. Marco Brambilla was in a room a floor beneath this level, but the door was heavily guarded.

Myrddin would need a big distraction if he had any hope of getting into that room.

8

CONSTANTINOPLE, 327 A.D.

Derog the Banished.

He wasn't always known by that name. Merlin remembered him as a young man eager to learn the mystical arts.

Merlin had sought to start a community of gifted people who, with his help, could be shaped into something better. Looking back now, he realized that he must have grown weary of fighting the dark tide that was the accursed all by himself. So, he had hoped to find others of like mind to join him.

Derog had quickly grasped the fundamentals of the magical arts and had become Merlin's best student. He'd master spells immediately without needing repeated instruction, and Merlin understood that he had a prodigy on his hands. But Derog's success had blinded him to his student's true nature until it was too late.

In a fit of rage, Derog had cast blood magic against a young woman who spurned his attentions. In exchange for great power, he offered her as a sacrifice to an evil entity.

Merlin was able to stop the ritual and banished the entity before it entered this plane, but he was too late to save the young woman.

Derog had been crestfallen and begged for forgiveness, saying she had cheated on him and his actions were caused by jealousy.

Merlin chose mercy and spared Derog's life. But as punishment, he broke Derog's core, the center of his magic, making it impossible for him to cast spells.

Now it seemed Derog had found a way to practice magic again and had reverted to his old ways of ritual sacrifice.

"We are here," Calisto whispered.

Merlin shook himself out of his reverie and studied his environment.

One of Calisto's informants reported strange happenings in a house on the outskirts of Constantinople. Apparently, chanting could be heard from the house at night, and the bleating of goats being slaughtered often kept the informant's family awake.

The night was dark, but Merlin cast a spell to boost his senses. It didn't cost much essence to maintain. The simple spell made it possible to see and hear better than an average human being, but it also had an unwelcomed effect. Merlin's sense of smell was also enhanced.

He caught a whiff of sweat and musk from Calisto. The reek of male hormones that wafted from the protector assaulted his nose, mingling with the damp smell of the earth. But worst of all was the scent of blood coming from the small wooden shack some meters ahead of him.

"I smell blood," he whispered.

Merlin couldn't be sure if it was animal or human blood, but the distinct metallic smell was unmistakable as it filled the air around him.

He reached out with his senses and felt the presence of several people in the shack. He held up four fingers to Calisto, who nodded and started creeping stealthily toward the dwelling, his short sword clasped in his hand. Merlin followed silently behind him. He cancelled any noise he made with another spell, and they reached the side of the shack without being detected.

Calisto took a deep breath and then kicked the wooden door in. He rushed into the room to see four figures in hoods glance in his direction in surprise. Merlin entered a moment later and released an air spell.

Although Merlin had the ability to control all the elements, he had learnt over time that he had more of an affinity for air. Air spells came easier to him and cost him little or no essence.

Four ropes of air wrapped around the hooded figures and ensnared them. The figures struggled in vain to escape as Merlin looked around the small room.

The group was stood around a crude circle of blood with a pentagram inscribed in its center. Merlin would never understand why humans thought they could bargain with demons and dark entities. The spirits that answered blood spells were liars looking to devour any human stupid enough to attempt a covenant with them.

Calisto pulled the hoods from the figures' heads, revealing four startled faces.

"Where is Derog?" Merlin asked.

Merlin saw a look of recognition flash across the faces of the four men, but they remained silent. They were amateurs who thought they could play in the big leagues. Their type was a dime a dozen and no match for people of higher intellect.

"I can get the information from your minds, but I assure you, it will be extremely painful," Merlin threatened. The men remained defiant and stared back unflinchingly.

He was reluctant to cast a mind-penetration spell on the four men. The spell was painful, unreliable, and likely to leave the men catatonic for days, if not longer.

"Do you think Derog cares about you? He doesn't. He only cares about himself," Merlin sneered.

"Our master shows us the way," one of the men said. "His knowledge will pave the way for the return of our god."

"You are too late. The ritual is complete," another added.

Merlin frowned. The amateurish circle on the

ground was clearly part of a low-level ritual meant to send a plea to the nether realm. By itself, the ritual was a waste, as anybody with an ounce of faith could resist the effects of the spell. Though the ritual had been completed, the spell was weak. It wouldn't be able to attract the attention of...

No!

"What have you done?" Merlin demanded.

One of the four men started laughing.

"It is too late. Our god arises," he said.

Merlin walked to the laughing man and stopped inches from his face. He resisted the urge to tighten the band of air and crack the man's ribs.

"What's going on?" Calisto asked, speaking for the first time since they entered the shack. He was a willing and useful ally, but he deferred to Merlin when it came to all things magic.

"I miscalculated," Merlin answered.

The ritual was weak, just like the last one he had seen, but, when combined...

"They used small, insignificant circles to form a larger one. Small enough that I wouldn't suspect their goal."

"So, what are we up against?" Calisto asked after a pause.

"Something nasty."

Could it be? Merlin wondered.

He reached out with his senses. Now that he knew what to look out for, it was easy to spot. Five small circles that combined to form a large pentagram with the palace at its center.

"We need to get back to the palace," Merlin said.

"Why?"

"Their real target is one of the royal family."

Merlin and Calisto rushed out of the shack. Behind them, the sound of the ensnared men's maniacal laughter filled the night. Merlin kept the ropes of air intact; he would release them once the palace guards arrived to escort the ritualists to the dungeon.

Ever since Marius escaped from prison, Queen Helena found it hard to fall asleep at night. She kept thinking about how close the accursed had come to succeeding during their previous onslaught.

Calisto increased the protection around her section of the palace, but Helena still couldn't relax, even with so many guards around.

Her only solace was in reading manuscripts containing messages and accounts from the life of Jesus Christ.

Emperor Constantine had outlawed unsanctioned gatherings, so she couldn't even meet with her Christian brethren in fellowship.

Helena felt boxed in.

If her son didn't relax the law impeding fellowships, the accursed will already have won.

Queen Helena sat by her night table and tilted the scroll in her hands toward the lamp on the edge of the table, a letter attributed to the apostle Paul, written to the Ephesians. She had been studying it for a while and enjoyed the sense of peace it brought her.

The lamp's wick flickered, and a cold sensation flowed through Helena's body and soul.

She shivered.

Although the night was cool, there wasn't any wind or a breeze to account for the sudden cold that gripped her bones.

A sense of unease settled over her, and she looked around the room slowly, trying to still her rapidly beating heart.

There was nothing there with her. She was alone. Or as alone as she could see…

She opened her mouth to call out to the guard stationed outside her door but hesitated.

What would she say to the guard? That she was afraid of a little breeze?

She could just imagine the smirk she would receive from him. While the praetorian guards were tough and loyal, they could also be cynical and smug.

Helena decided to swallow her pride as an over-whelming sense of danger enveloped her. She opened her mouth to call out when the attack came.

Some…presence crushed her into silence. She felt a weight pressing on her chest and groaned in agony, toppling backward and falling to the floor.

Sharp claws raked at her mind, trying to invade her being.

Queen Helena screamed silently.

Pain flushed through her pores and battered her soul.

She could sense her life ebbing away. She heard a faint knocking on the door and prayed the guard would enter.

Help me! Helena cried within her soul.

She tried to move her hands, but pain flooded her insides and she almost blacked out. Helena willed her mind to remain awake, as she somehow understood that she couldn't afford to pass out. Rebelling against the pain, she grunted and moved her fingers slowly to her thigh.

It felt like her mind would shatter into a thousand pieces from the effort, but she kept inching her fingers upward. She touched the nail strapped to her thigh and immediately felt the attack ease off. The pain subsided, and Helena took a deep breath to gather her strength. Yelling in defiance, she pulled the nail out and stabbed the air above her.

A howl filled the room as the invisible entity jumped off her. Everything shook as the entity roared with anger, and Helena gulped air into her bruised throat. She heard her bedroom door break open, and Calisto and Merlin rushed in.

Merlin started chanting, and light burst from his hand. The light struck the air above Helena, and she saw the shimmering outline of the being that had attacked her.

"What the hell is that?" Calisto shouted. Following his instincts to protect the queen, he ran and plunged his sword into the entity.

Queen Helena saw the entity raise its hand and swing at Calisto.

"Watch out!" she shouted.

The blow struck Calisto hard, and he was blasted against the wall. Merlin continued to hit the entity with light from his hand.

The entity continued to shimmer, its features becoming clearer. Helena gasped as a grotesque face turned in her direction and howled in rage. The entity stepped toward her, and she backed away in fear.

Calisto struggled to his feet and steadied himself against the wall. Pain racked his body as he took in a deep breath. He bent down and picked up his sword, noticing that its tip was melted, probably from when it had pierced the being. Calisto saw the creature advance slowly toward Queen Helena, and he charged again.

He swung at the entity with his sword, and this time, he struck the beast's side. He winced as the force of the blow vibrated through his arm. The creature turned and took a swing back.

He parried the blow but, to his amazement, his blade barely left a scratch on the beast's arm. The force pushed Calisto back, and he found himself against the same wall he'd been slammed into moments ago.

Merlin released the light spell and quickly cast a binding spell.

He and Calisto had hurried back to the palace as soon as he understood the magnitude of the ritualists' spell.

They were dealing with a higher demon from the nether realm, and a straightforward light spell wouldn't be enough to stop it.

Merlin watched as the binding spell struck the entity and froze it into place. The creature sneered and turned its eyes in his direction. He could feel the hate for humanity that rippled from the demon as it struggled against the binding spell. The spell held, but Merlin knew it wouldn't last for long. He could already feel the strain of containing a higher demon.

"You need to use the nail!" Merlin shouted.

Queen Helena hesitated.

Fear had gripped her when Calisto was thrown against the wall. She had seen him hold his side and knew he was hurt badly, otherwise, he would not have let it show. She saw the demon turn in her direction and instinctively retreated. To her amazement, Calisto struggled to his feet.

Helena wanted to scream at him to remain still. She trusted him to handle any human threat, but what stood before them now was far from human.

She clutched the nail to her chest as Calisto launched himself at the beast. The entity struck, and he stumbled back again. Helena saw Merlin stretch out his hand, and suddenly the beast froze.

"You need to use the nail!" Merlin shouted.

Helena tried to summon the courage to still her shaking limbs and take a step toward the entity. She saw the strain on Merlin's face as he struggled with the beast's strength.

"Now!" he shouted.

The force of the word propelled Helena forward. She heard herself screaming as she stepped up to the beast and drove the nail into its back.

The beast's howls shook the room again. She felt plaster raining down on her face from the ceiling and lifted a hand to shield her eyes from the dust.

She fell back, still holding on to the foot nail.

The creature looked in her direction and saw the nail in her hand. It howled again and rushed for the window, crashing through it headfirst.

Silence filled the bedroom.

Calisto staggered to Queen Helena's side. "Are you hurt?"

His voice sounded raspy, and Helena wondered if he'd cracked a rib when he hit the wall. She shook her head as she got to her feet. Merlin walked over to Calisto and placed a hand on his shoulder. Helena's assumption had been correct. After a pause, Calisto took a deep breath without pain and nodded to Merlin in thanks.

"What was that?" Calisto asked.

"A high demon. The spate of pagan worship was intended to bring that demon into our realm," Merlin explained.

"Why?"

"It's obvious, isn't it?" Merlin turned to Helena. "You were the demon's target. What I don't understand is why the accursed would resort to making pacts with demons."

"Unless this isn't their doing?" Calisto remembered the words of the four men they caught earlier. "Who is Derog?" he asked.

Merlin remained silent, and Helena used the opportunity to right the chair that had tumbled over when the demon had attacked her. She collapsed into it as she waited for Merlin's response.

"He used to be an apprentice of mine," he replied quietly.

"Then isn't it possible that this is his doing?" Calisto asked.

"No."

Merlin was clearly reluctant to dredge up painful memories, but Calisto wouldn't relent. Not that she didn't agree with her protector's line of questioning.

"How can you be so sure?" Calisto demanded.

"It can't be Derog because Derog can't practice magic anymore. I took that away from him."

"And he was your only apprentice?" Calisto asked.

"The only one left alive," Merlin answered warily.

Derog was broken, stripped of any ability to perform magic. No one could mend or repair a broken core. Derog would never be able to practice magic again.

Merlin wondered if he had been foolish to leave his apprentice alive.

A true sorcerer could learn to adapt to any situation.

Could Derog have somehow adapted and found a way to circumvent his restrictions? The man had been a genius. Could he have found a way to do the impossible?

9

Mark was right.

He saw the man standing beside the leader raise his rifle and take aim at Gen. The moment he did, Mark burst into action. His spiritual senses expanded, and the world slowed down around him.

The bullet burst from the muzzle of the gun, travelling through the air slowly like it was moving through treacle. Mark was already swinging. His sword throbbed in his hand as it bit into the bullet, slicing it in two.

The world kicked back into motion, and he saw the confused looks.

The leader grunted and signalled to his men to attack. Eight men raised their FN SCARs and pointed them at Mark, Gen, and Lucilius.

Gen saw Mark move, and the world seemed to skip. She didn't know what he'd done, but she had felt the air ripple in front of her, blowing strands of her hair across her face. The man who had raised his weapon was staring at the gun with a dumb look on his face. She concluded that he had shot her, and Mark must have intercepted the bullet with his sword.

She had seen her protector pull off that impossible feat before, so she wasn't dumbstruck like the attackers. The nail in her hand pulsed. Suddenly, she was swept away by a vision.

Gen blinked and looked around. She seemed to be in an outdoor arena, but the place was deserted. The heat from the sand penetrated her shoes, even though the day was long spent and the sun was setting. Gen heard a grunt and turned to see a teenager holding a shield and a bastard sword. The young man grunted as he struck at an invisible opponent.

"I see you are still practicing, Calisto," said a deep voice from behind her. She turned around to see a beefy man holding a sword and wearing nothing but a loincloth.

The young man—Calisto—didn't answer, just continued thrusting his sword.

"You need to make use of your shield, too," the beefy man said. "It is meant to protect you from the enemy's attacks," he said, jumping swiftly to attack as he did.

Calisto was forced to protect himself. There was a loud clang as the short sword met the metal shield, and the beefy man grinned.

"Good. Hold it at shoulder height. Not too low, or your opponent can skewer your eyes, and not too high that you don't see the attack."

He continued attacking, but Calisto managed to block all the attacks with his shield.

Gen felt the nail vibrate in her fist, and the vision faded. She now understood what she was meant to do.

It was time she became a shield.

Gen snapped back to the present and saw the whole line of attackers raise their guns and take aim at her, Mark, and Lucilius. She didn't know if Mark would be able to stop the barrage of bullets about to come their way, but at that instant, she sensed what she had to do.

The nail continued to vibrate in her grasp, and she took two steps forward. Ignoring the startled look on Mark's face, she thrust out her hand and braced herself.

The nail hummed as the men started shooting, but the bullets didn't go far. Instead, they struck what looked like a transparent, round shield. The air rippled at the points of impact, and Gen grunted as the force pushed her back.

Mark was shocked by Gen's unexpected display of power, but he recovered quickly and moved in on the strike teams. He aimed for the leader but had to duck when he saw one of the men aim at him and pull the trigger. The bullet whisked past his head, and then Mark was on top of the leader.

The man reacted quickly, trying to step back to create space to use his weapon, but Mark anticipated the move and swiped up with his sword.

His enchanted sword was created through the combined might of the greatest wizard to ever live and a real-live angel. Together, they merged two of the nails of power with a broken sword. What they made was one of a kind, but the sword had one limitation—it couldn't harm living flesh. Anything else was fair game.

The leader of the strike team tried to block Mark's blow before realizing he'd made a mistake. Mark's sword sliced through his gun and sheared it in half. To the man's credit, he tried to counter by bringing out a knife from behind his back, but Mark used his momentum to slam his elbow into his exposed ribs.

The leader grunted and fell to his knees. Mark turned to face another member of the team who had his gun trained on him, about to open fire. Gen intercepted just in time, stopping the bullets with her invisible shield. Mark felt his sword humming in resonance with the nail in Gen's hand. Without fully knowing what he was doing, Mark linked his essence to the nail. He was acting purely from instinct, but it felt right. He could sense the nail and use that to connect better with Gen.

Mark and Gen became a whirlwind at the center of the strike team, and in no time, two more men had dropped to the floor. The remaining men spread out, trying to find a way to corner them. With their focus on the nail bearer and her protector, the attackers made the grave mistake of forgetting about Lucilius.

Lucilius pulled the pistol from the holster on his hip. The fight erupted with almost no warning. He saw Gen do something with the nail in her hand just before the bullets started ripping from the strike team's weapons. But instead of hitting their targets, the bullets somehow stopped mid-air.

The attackers scattered, trying to corner Mark and Gen. That was when Lucilius started picking them off one by one.

He struggled with indecision for a second, then made up his mind not to go for headshots. Over the months he had been training with Mark, Lucilius had come to understand that, although he was a weapons master, he was proficient at any means of combat, including hand-to-hand.

Lucilius had shot attackers in their legs before the remaining men even figured out that they didn't have the advantage anymore. It was now three against three.

Josephine didn't understand why she'd been ordered to stay in the house when she could, in fact, be very useful. She'd proven herself in the fight against Asmodeus and could handle herself with her time-reversal ability, so she didn't get Mark's reasoning. She was basically babysitting O'Neal and Isabella.

Isabella flinched anytime she heard a gunshot, which made Josephine want to head out of the house and go help the others even more, consequences be damned.

Instead, she prowled up and down the sitting room like a caged animal.

"You know, statistically, Gen, Mark, and Lucilius stand a fair chance of surviving the encounter," O'Neal said, trying to pacify her.

Josephine paused her pacing and gave the former doctor her attention. "I know they are capable, and that's why I wanted to be out there and not stuck in here." "Also, there is the slim chance that Genesis Isherwood will fail and be killed," the doctor said.

Josephine growled in frustration and headed for the door.

"Mark said we're backup, Jose," Isabella cautioned.

Josephine snorted. "We're the kids the adults don't want around when they want to have fun."

"Have fun? You call what is happening out there having fun? I'm scared out of my wits." Isabella brought her hands up in frustration and shook her head.

"It could be considered fun to fight an inferior force that cannot contend with your power, like the famous ant and elephant analogy," O'Neal smiled, happy he could understand the conversation for once.

"Maybe fun wasn't the right word, but we're not helpless. We can contribute," Josephine tried explaining.

"What can we do that Mark and Gen can't do better? They're virtually superheroes," Isabella said.

"And what about Lucilius?" Josephine countered.

"What about him?" Isabella asked.

"He doesn't have any abilities anymore, but he's out there."

"He has combat experience, having lived for eons," O'Neal offered.

Josephine glared at them. She had to admit she was worried. Not for Mark and Gen—she didn't think anything could get close enough to harm Gen with Mark alive, and Mark was a force of nature. They were safe. Her fear was for Lucilius. She wondered when her feelings for the immortal had turned from disgust to worry.

Lucilius had been sent to kill her, and if not for Mark intervening at Gen's behest, Josephine would have survived terminal cancer only to die at his hand. Now she had seen another side of him, a side that made her want to spend time in his presence.

She learnt that he was fiercely loyal and greatly misunderstood.

Yes, she wanted to be out there facing the danger with the others so she could watch his back.

The fight ended as swiftly as it had started. Mark held his sword to the neck of the attackers' leader, and the man tried not to flinch.

Mark knew the sword wouldn't cut him—it would simply pass through him harmlessly—but the man didn't know that, and he wasn't about to enlighten him. He had tried to kill them, after all.

Gen walked up and took her place by Mark's side. He was surprised by her actions during the fight and could tell from her smile that she was pleased to have helped.

"What was that with the nail?" he asked. "I've never seen you do that before."

Gen gave a tiny shrug. "I don't really understand it myself. You know when you have a feeling that you've been under-utilizing something? That's the feeling I've been getting with the foot nail recently."

"We'll talk about that later."

Mark turned his attention back to the soldiers now kneeling before him. The men were bruised and beaten, and some had gunshot wounds in their legs. Though their lives were not in immediate danger, they would need medical treatment soon.

Lucilius watched over them holding one of the assault rifles he'd confiscated from the attackers.

Mark was facing somewhat of a dilemma. He

couldn't kill the men. Not just because Gen wouldn't stand for it, but also because he didn't believe he had the heart to do it. But they couldn't just allow them to go free.

He decided to try and get as much information from them as he could.

"Why are you after Gen?" Mark asked sternly.

The men remained stoic in their silence. He wasn't surprised. They were special forces; they wouldn't break easily, even under torture.

"Where did you serve?" he said, trying a different tactic. Their expression didn't change, but Mark's spiritual essence detected a slight shift in the leader's center. This was the way to get to them.

"I did a tour in Iraq myself," Mark said. "I was a member of Task Force 88."

This time, the men couldn't hide their surprise, and the leader looked up at Mark with a glimmer of respect in his eyes.

"Those boys did good," he said with a nod.

"I'm not going to be waterboarding anyone or using any form of torture," Mark said. "But I can get the information I need from you. So why don't you save yourselves some discomfort and tell me what I need to know?" Mark hoped the men would see reason.

Without Myrddin around, they couldn't extract information from the men's minds directly. Gen had the ability to detect lies, but that would only be helpful if Mark asked the right questions and the men felt talkative.

"I can only give you my name and rank," the leader said. "Anything else, you'd have to pry out of me." He looked up at Mark as he continued talking. "And I can assure you: we don't break easily."

"That's a start, anyway. So, who do I have the pleasure of talking with?" Mark asked.

"My name is Sergeant Patrick Anderson. These are my men, but they won't be introducing themselves."

Mark took Gen by the elbow and led her a few feet away from the men, leaving Lucilius to watch over them.

"What's the play?" he asked when he was sure they wouldn't be overheard.

"I thought that was up to you. As long as we don't do anything to them that would hurt our consciences, you can carry on."

"Torturing them wouldn't hurt my conscience, not after they tried to kill you."

"No form of torture," Gen insisted. "And I know you want to keep your options open, Mark, but I also see your heart. You wouldn't allow anyone to hurt them either."

Mark sighed, and they walked back to the men.

"Today's your lucky day. You get one free pass. I'll be on the lookout for you, and if I ever catch so much as a glimpse of any of you again, take it from me; you wouldn't like what happens."

The leader looked up at him in surprise. It quickly turned into suspicion, but Mark meant what he'd said. He nodded at Lucilius, and the ex-immortal backed away from the men.

"You can leave, but I'm sure you'll understand if you don't get your weapons back," Mark told the men.

The leader slowly got to his feet. When Mark didn't attack, the rest of the men got up too, helping their wounded shuffle back to their vehicles.

"Was that a good decision?" Lucilius asked as they watched the men drive away.

"Maybe not. But that doesn't mean we'll sit idly by. We know what they look like, and we know someone's after Gen. We may not know who our enemy is, but we're ready for them now."

"Could they have anything to do with that You-Tuber?" Gen wondered aloud.

"Russell Patel?" Mark asked.

"Yes. Surely it can't be a coincidence that he starts fermenting trouble on the internet, and next thing, we get attacked."

"Then we need to pay this Russell character a visit," Lucilius suggested.

Mark turned and followed Gen back to the house. He wondered what a YouTuber could have to do with the attack. Were they connected, or was Gen in more danger than they thought?

10

The door from the balcony led to what appeared to be a guest room. Although the bedroom was large, it felt crowded with a massive wardrobe that stood against one wall and a bed that took up the remaining space. Myrddin had to walk sideways to get to the other end of the room. He leaned against the wall and slumped to the floor, taking a moment to rest and cycle essence back into his center.

Most magic practitioners needed to sit cross-legged or find a meditative pose while restoring their essence, but Myrddin could make do with any position. Sitting in a meditative pose would allow him to be more focused and cycle faster, but he could start cycling essence from his being to his center even while slumped against the wall.

He kept his senses pushed out, but not too far. *Better safe than sorry.*

The spell would cause a trembling in the ether if anybody tried to open the door, and Myrddin would sense it even if he were distracted or asleep. So, he would know the moment someone entered the bedroom, and he was sure he could conjure an illusion spell quickly enough to hide himself if that happened. Since he was stationary and only needed to blend in with the wall behind him, he was confident he wouldn't be caught unawares.

Shutting his eyes, he softly chanted and cast a spell at the bedroom door.

Having secured himself as best as he could, Myrddin relaxed and fell into a meditative state.

Myrddin woke up with a start. Someone was opening the bedroom door. He quickly cast an illusion spell and faded into the grey wall behind him just as a man stepped into the room.

The man glanced around the room. He was all muscle, bundled up in the black suit that seemed to be the official dress code for bodyguards, Secret Service agents, and security personnel the world over.

"Section 4A all clear," the man said, holding a finger to his earpiece. He turned around and left the room, closing the door behind him with a soft click.

Myrddin released the illusion spell and frowned. He had regained almost half of his essence during his short nap. He was still too depleted and, though he didn't expect to be at full throttle after such a brief rest, less than half of his power was way below the margin. Myrddin shook off the doubts that tried to infect his mind and got to his feet. He reached out with his essence to scan the room next door.

Though it was getting late, Marco Brambilla was still in the same room he'd been in when Myrddin had arrived outside the villa. It didn't mean much, but Myrddin hadn't lived to his ripe old age by being unprepared for all contingencies.

He conjured a shield over his body and cast the illusion spell again.

Myrddin opened the door and peered into a narrow corridor. He whispered a chant, and footprints appeared on the carpet in front of him. He followed them stealthily through the corridor until he came to a staircase.

Faint whispers grew louder as he crept slowly down the stairs, prepared for anything. Still cloaked by his illusion spell, Myrddin reached the bottom of the stairs and halted. There were over ten security guards patrolling the hallway in front of the room Marco Brambilla was in.

He had prepared for this. Knowing Marco would be heavily guarded, he had come up with a simple solution to get past security. Myrddin chanted internally and released the spell he'd prepared for this moment.

Right on cue, the guards' earpieces crackled to life. "We have a situation on the balcony. Two intruders detected."

The men tensed up and raised their guns. He smiled and activated the second part of his plan. Suddenly, the ratatat of gunfire exploded over the guards" earpieces. Myrddin's spell only affected the earpieces of the men he could see. Casting the spell over the whole house or villa would have been detrimental to his plan, as the noise and confusion would likely have caused all the guards to converge in Marco Brambilla's room to protect him.

One of the guards motioned for half of the men to remain while the other half followed him as he ran for the balcony.

A few seconds later, the door opened, and a lanky guard stepped into the hallway.

"What's going on?" he asked.

"Not sure, but Crawford took some men to check the balcony. We got a report of some intruders."

The lanky guard frowned and turned around to go back into the room. Myrddin knew he wouldn't get another opportunity. He sped toward the door, weaving around the remaining guards, using a little air spell to hover inches above the ground. He just managed to float into the room before the lanky guard shut the door again.

Myrddin softly touched down on the carpet inside. From the corner, he turned around and surveyed the room, careful not to make a sound. It was a study with a bookshelf lining one of the walls and a large executive desk in the center. Behind the desk, Marco Brambilla leaned back in a plush office chair, a cigar held loosely between his fingers. In addition to the lanky bodyguard, there were two other men in the room.

Marco Brambilla was a huge, middle-aged man with a thick, muscular body. He exhaled a cloud of smoke toward the ceiling, then turned to Myrddin and stared him straight in the eyes.

"Good to see you."

Marco spoke with a heavy accent that revealed his Italian heritage. Myrddin returned Marco's stare with a baffled look. There was no way he could see through the illusion, yet it was obvious that he was staring straight at him. Myrddin took a few steps toward the door, and Marco's eyes tracked his movement. The lanky guard left his position by one of the bookshelves and moved to stand in front of the door. The other two men also got to their feet, both sporting automatic weapons.

What is happening?

"I do not know who you are. You are strong. Your magic strong," Marco said in slightly strained English.

Myrddin ignored him for the moment and reached out with his essence. He didn't hold back, allowing his power to wash over the room. Marco flinched as Myrddin's essence slammed into him, but the remaining three men were ignorant of anything happening. The essence hit the room's walls and rebounded like a wave returning to the sea.

That should be impossible, Myrddin thought.

He took a closer look at the walls and noticed they were glowing with a golden sheen.

Can this be real?

He'd heard of gold obsidian but had never seen it. It was generally believed to be a myth, a legendary element with the power to negate magic.

"You see it, no?" Marco bellowed with a laugh. "I am right. You are very strong. No one senses the wall, not even me."

Myrddin had walked into a trap. He quickly attempted an air spell to create some batons, but it fizzled out, leaving nothing but sparks radiating from his hands.

"The walls. They drain all magic. I see you flying into the veranda, but not before." Marco stood up, and Myrddin saw that he was even larger than he'd initially thought. The man was a mountain, and Myrddin wondered why he even needed body-guards. He looked big enough to handle himself in a fight. But, then again, size was no match for bullets.

"Who are you?" Marco demanded.

Myrddin analyzed his chances and decided that the odds were definitely not in his favour. Without his magic, he wasn't sure he could take on four men, especially not when one of them looked like he could snap Myrddin in half without breaking a sweat.

"My name is Melvin Gourdeau," Myrddin finally said.

"Ah, you are an American. Good. I practice my English, yes?"

"Actually, I'm Canadian."

"Po-tay-to, po-tah-to, si? I get the idiom right?" Marco asked with a smile.

Why was he being friendly? Myrddin had snuck into Marco's villa with obviously hostile intentions, yet here the man was, almost offering him tea and practicing his terrible English. He decided to be upfront. If Marco wanted to act like the nice host, Myrddin wasn't complaining.

"You sold an item to Lorenzo Lamas."

"Lorenzo? Who is that?" Marco turned to the lanky man blocking the door, and Myrddin decided that he was probably not a bodyguard like the others. Maybe a personal assistant?

The man shrugged, and Marco turned back to Myrddin.

"I do not know any Lorenzo. He says he buys from me?"

"Not exactly. He bought the item from the curator of the National Museum."

"Ah, Maria Blupoint. A reasonable woman. She tells me about you. We trade. Information for information."

Myrddin couldn't figure Marco out. He decided to trust his instincts and go with the flow.

"Okay. I'll go first. Do you have the original crown of thorns?"

Marco tilted his head to the side and made a so-so gesture with his hand.

"You sell Maria a fake nail. Do you have original?"

Myrddin smiled and emulated the so-so gesture with his hand. Just like that, Marco dropped his easygoing act, and the real man loomed before him.

Marco moved faster than Myrddin thought possible, crossing the space between them in an instant. Myrddin felt bands of iron wrap around his throat. As he sputtered and choked, he realized that it was Marco's fingers that were wrapped around his neck. He felt his body leave the ground and kicked his feet ineffectually as he flayed about.

Marco released him and he dropped to the floor, swallowing and wincing at the raw pain in his throat.

"We go again. How you get the nail of power?" Marco asked, congenial once more.

"It was fake," Myrddin croaked.

"I know, but no one knows of the nail. How you create...eh..." Marco snapped his fingers a few times as he tried to find the right word.

"So parlare in Italiano," Myrddin said. Marco grinned like a child in a candy shop.

"You speak Italian?" Marco asked in Italian.

"I just said so."

"Good. This will make things quicker. How did you know about the nail? No one knows about the nail of power."

"I am a collector of antiquities, just like you. I bought the nail some years ago, but like you, I found out it was a fake. I kept it because, like you just mentioned, no one knows about the nail."

"I think you're lying, or not telling the complete truth."

"Neither are you, Marco Brambilla."

Myrddin glanced around as they spoke, looking for a way to escape the study. Marco smiled and moved back to his seat. The leather chair squeaked in protest against his weight as he swivelled from side to side.

"We will keep you as a guest till you can trust me enough to tell me where the real nail is," he said, flashing a smile that Myrddin didn't reciprocate. The moment he left the room, his powers would return, and Myrddin assured himself he would turn the tables then. He now understood why he had been getting those headaches and had difficulty casting since he flew into the villa; the gold obsidian must have been affecting his powers.

Marco opened a drawer, fished out a pair of manacles, and dropped them on his desk with a clang. Myrddin's heart sank. The manacles were connected by a chain of pure gold, and he didn't have to be a wizard to know that he was looking at more gold obsidian.

"You will put this on," Marco said, that persistent, irritating smile still plastered on his face. Myrddin wished he could conjure an air whip and slash that smug look off his face.

"Can we talk about this?" Myrddin tried.

"Yes, after you've put the cuffs on."

From the corner of his eye, Myrddin saw the two, armed men now had their rifles pointed at him.

He walked to the desk and picked up the manacles, placed them over his wrists and clicked them shut one by one.

For the first time in his life, Myrddin was powerless.

11

Garth drummed his fingers on the steering wheel as he drove into the quaint little town of Dundurn. He rented a Corolla in Saskatoon, and the journey down had been pleasant, although on the dull side. He didn't mind; the peace and quiet gave him time to think and strategize.

William would be back, of that Garth was sure. But in what capacity, he had no way of knowing. If William returned to the Citadel and reported Garth's actions, he could be ex-communicated. Unlike other religious bodies or organizations, to the Citadel, ex-communication didn't mean banishment. It meant death.

A trial would be held in his absence, and he would be sentenced accordingly. Knowing the Citadel, the only thing that would give him an iota of avoiding capital punishment was if he could prove he had justifiable reasons for disregarding their orders. Garth didn't mind dying if it was for the right reasons. But he sure as hell wasn't going to die for the Citadel.

Garth had to bring in Lucilius, dead or alive.

He parked the Corolla on a deserted street beside a shop that read 'Mayfield's Bakery' and killed the engine. He got out of the car and looked around. Garth was about to pick a random door to knock on when he heard the crunch of boots on loose gravel.

He turned around to see a young-looking man wearing a sheriff's uniform. The sheriff already had his right hand above the gun holster on his hip.

"How may I help you, sir?" he asked politely. Despite the man's calm voice, Garth could see the tension in his posture.

"Just passing through," Garth offered.

"Could I see some identification, please?" Again, the sheriff was trying to act friendly, but Garth could see that he was anything but. He shrugged and dug into his back pocket for his wallet. When he looked back up, the sheriff had his gun aimed right at him.

"What's going on, Officer?"

"Show me your hands. Do it slowly."

Garth lifted his hand slowly, showing the wallet he'd fished out of his pocket.

"It's my wallet, Officer."

"I'll be the judge of that."

The sheriff turned him around and pushed him roughly against the trunk of the rental car. Garth reined in his anger as he patted him down and searched his pockets.

"I don't have any weapons on me, Officer."

Garth felt the officer release him, and he straightened up.

"What are you doing here, Mr....Armstrong?" the sheriff asked, peering at his license.

"Like I said, I'm just passing through. Thought I'd check on my friend from way back. Came here looking for directions."

The sheriff studied him thoughtfully, and Garth tried not to let his annoyance show on his face. Maybe there was a logical explanation for this treatment.

"Sorry about that, Mr. Armstrong. We've had quite a few incidences of vandalization and theft lately, so we're wary of strangers. As you can see, this is a small and peaceful town, and we'd like to keep it that way."

Garth nodded in acceptance and collected his wallet from the sheriff's outstretched hand.

"Where did you say your friend lived? Maybe I can give you directions."

"That would be great, Officer," Garth replied. He tried to remember the name of the place the informant said Lucilius was hiding.

"Eh, I'm looking for a ranch, the Triple 7 ranch."

No sooner had he spoken than the sheriff whipped out his gun for the second time. Garth could have knocked him out with his magic, but he didn't want to alert Lucilius of his presence.

"You are under arrest. Up against the car, spread your feet, and place your hands behind your back."

Garth couldn't believe his ears, but when he heard the sheriff cocking the gun in his hands, he was quick to comply.

Minutes later, he was sitting on the bare floor of the only cell in the small sheriff's office.

Just what is going on? he wondered as he stared through the bars and saw the sheriff dialling a number on his cellphone.

Gen watched the soldiers bundle into their cars and drive out of sight. She still had the nail clenched firmly in her hand. Its rough edges dug into her palm but didn't break the skin.

"You've been hiding things from me," Mark teased.

She knew what he meant. She was just as surprised as he must have been when the invisible shield sprang up.

She shrugged, bemused, and turned back toward the house.

Mark fell into step next to her while Lucilius trailed a few feet behind them.

"You didn't plan on that happening?" he asked, and Gen shook her head. She saw Mark grit his teeth and immediately realized her mistake.

"I really wasn't in danger, Mark."

"I thought you'd practiced creating that shield, and that was why you wanted to take a stand with me and Lucilius."

140

"And I'm glad I did. You know I hate it when you get to fight our adversaries alone. I can't stand idly by and watch you get hurt."

"I'm the protector Gen; it's kind of in the job description. You know you're too important for us to put in danger. These guys came specifically for you."

She reached out and clasped Mark's hand as they got close to the porch. "We're in this together. I think tonight shows that."

She was amazed at how well they had fought together. For a moment, they were perfectly in sync. She'd been able to predict his next move and knew when to cover his back. It had been...exhilarating. She heard Mark grunt and knew he must have sensed what she was talking about. Yes, it was dangerous for her to be that close to an attack, but if she hadn't joined Mark in the fight, they'd never have known the nail could be so much more.

The door opened, and a fuming Josephine stepped out with Isabella and O'Neal behind her.

"I agree with you," Mark told Josephine before she could say anything. Josephine's shoulders slumped in defeat. She had come out prepared to stand her ground in an argument, and Mark had just pulled the rug from under her feet.

Gen was glad when Mark had taken on the role of both her protector and the leader of the group. She remembered asking her granddad why he didn't want to lead. Myrddin had waved the question aside and said that Mark would be a perfect fit. She hadn't understood it then, but she could now see that Mark had grown into the position.

"We could have used your help tonight, Josephine, but I felt confident knowing that whatever threat managed to get by us would have you to contend with. That made me more focused because I didn't have to worry about you guys."

Gen thought Mark was laying it on a bit thick, but his statement seemed to pacify Josephine, as she relaxed her posture visibly. She smiled when she noticed the fleeting glance Josephine gave Lucilius, hoping that what she saw blossoming would mature into a perfect flower.

Lucilius had been struggling for a while with feelings of inadequacy. He did his best to keep those doubts caged in, but they were getting stronger, rattling at the bars of their prison in his mind and threatening to spill out into the world.

He missed who he used to be.

Not the bloodthirsty immortal that had savaged worlds and decimated kingdoms, no. He missed the power that came with his immortality. He missed the thrill of invincibility, knowing nothing could do him serious harm or kill him. Now he had to hide behind those that wielded power and try to make the best of the situation.

As they neared the house, he tuned out the whispers of the nail bearer and her protector.

He wondered for a moment if he'd made the right choice in choosing the light. His soul felt free but empty, devoid of purpose or goals. All his life, he'd hunted nail bearers in pursuit of his goal to gather the three nails of power.

He had thought the drive was his, but now he knew better. He was a puppet in another's hand. Someone else had been pulling his strings. The reality of it dawned on him when Asmodeus had come into this world.

Yes, Lucilius had served a master, but he'd thought that his master had given him free rein to do whatever he'd pleased. It was humbling to be told he'd been nothing but a pawn the whole time.

Lucilius reined in his emotions as the door of the house opened, and Josephine rushed out. He felt her anger at being shoved to the sidelines and understood.

What if he was still a puppet? Had he just chosen another master who would pull his strings in whatever direction she pleased without any consideration for his feelings?

Maybe it was time to step out on his own. That was what he'd originally intended—before circumstances pushed him to throw in his lot with Gen and her merry band of righteous characters.

Josephine glanced at Lucilius and saw the troubled look on his face.

She didn't understand why she felt the need to comfort him, but she saw him as she would a loved one who was at risk of suicide. Lucilius tried to appear calm and collected, but she sensed he was swimming in uncertainty. Having considered taking her life when she was suffering from cancer, she could recognize the same feeling coming off Lucilius. Not that he seemed suicidal, exactly, but there was a desperation to him that did not bode well; like he was at a turning point in his life. And Josephine didn't want him to make the wrong decision.

She shook her head at herself as she headed back inside the house. She didn't know what she felt for the former accursed. She should feel hate, as Lucilius had tried to kill her and would have succeeded if it hadn't been for Mark. But she didn't. Instead, she felt a kind of camaraderie with the ex-immortal. She knew what it was to be lost and have your whole foundation shaken or destroyed. She lost everything when the cancer had reached its terminal stage and had felt so alone. She believed she understood what Lucilius was going through.

12

The lanky assistant led Myrddin down a flight of stairs and out of the main house. The other two guards were watching him like a hawk, but he didn't give them a second glance.

He needed to get out of the manacles, but try as he might, he couldn't force out even a trickle of essence. He hated not being connected to the well of spiritual energy that rested at the center of his being.

The assistant led him to a small building not far from the main house, pulled a key from his pocket, and unlocked the door. The wooden door creaked as it swung open, and the musty smell of disuse assaulted Myrddin's nostrils. One of the guards shoved him into the room from behind, and then the door slammed shut behind him.

A couple of minutes passed before Myrddin's eyes adjusted to the sudden gloom. There was a small table with a chair near him, and a single mattress lay on the floor against the far wall.

He noticed a switch on the wall beside the door and flipped it on. He squinted at the sudden brightness but could now also see a wardrobe in the corner.

What is this place?

The furniture looked old, and the room smelled like it hadn't been used in years.

Myrddin dropped his eyes to his hands and raised them in front of his face. He studied the manacles that shackled not only his hands, but his powers as well. The gold obsidian shimmered, and Myrddin wondered how the ore had been processed. Black obsidian could be cut and even crushed, just like any other piece of rock, but it couldn't be forged.

Is gold obsidian different?

He tried to remember what he'd seen in Marco's study. The walls had given off a golden glow, which he surmised came from the gold obsidian, and Marco had said as much. Though powerful enough to block magic, Myrddin guessed that gold obsidian would break like any other material if enough force was applied to it.

Myrddin looked around for anything he could potentially use to damage the manacles, but the room was bare except for the mattress, wardrobe, table, and chair. He walked to the table and ran his hands across its surface. He leaned forward, putting all his weight on the table, and though it creaked, it didn't budge. He held his manacled hands above the edge of the table and took a deep breath. He brought the chains down hard, and a piece of the tabletop broke off under the force of his swing. Hoping the blow had damaged the gold obsidian, he tried snapping the manacles, but they wouldn't budge. He strained until pain shot through his wrists, but the metal still held.

Myrddin grunted in frustration and channelled energy into the manacles. He watched as his essence bled away, not stopping until he felt the last of his power being sucked into the manacles. Still, the gold chains held firm.

Myrddin sank into the chair, defeated, realizing that this time, he might just be in over his head.

After the arrest, the sheriff hadn't said a word to him; he had only made the one call that Garth couldn't quite overhear.

He could have escaped anytime he wanted, but he didn't want the law after him as well as the Citadel. He decided to wait for the right opportunity to make his move, and the end of the day seemed like a good time.

He rubbed the ring on his left middle finger. It was his reward for graduating at the top of his class at the Citadel Training Institute. It was made from a special metal that could store essence and, in rare cases, spells. Right now, the ring was a godsend.

The sheriff switched off the lights and left the police station without looking back. As Garth heard the click of a key turning in the lock, he got to his feet and gripped the bars of the holding cell with both hands. He could break through by creating a shield between two bars and expanding it, or he could just pick the lock. Most people thought of shields as round or rectangular, and while they were typically right, Garth specialized in creating shields of any shape.

He allowed his essence to seep into the keyhole and created a small oblong shield. Then, he expanded the shield, leaving it soft and malleable so that it would contort around the lock's mechanism. With a flick of his finger, he twisted and grinned when a soft click sounded, and the cell gate swung open.

Candice wished she had the magic to make her look more intimidating. With her petite figure, she looked like a victim or prey, which was aggravating. All her life, she'd had to work twice as hard as her taller, stronger peers.

She couldn't deny that having the physique of a pretty young woman came in handy when dealing with the opposite sex, but it also meant that people often looked down on her.

And that made her very angry.

That was why she didn't feel the slightest bit of remorse when her bodyguard snapped the finger of the National Museum's curator, Maria Blupoint.

When she contacted Ms. Blupoint, she had refused to meet with her. So, Candice took the initiative and approached her at the museum, but the woman had been rude, brushing off Candice's attempts at civility with a condescending air.

She didn't look so condescending anymore. Candice heard a muffled scream from the curator as another finger broke.

"We can do this all night, Ms. Blupoint. All I need from you is a name, and I'll be out of your hair and your home."

The curator struggled to say something through the napkin that was shoved into her mouth. The chair she was tied to squeaked as she shook in pain.

Candice sighed as she looked around the neat, clean kitchen. The curator's home was small but well-cared for. She ran her finger across the shiny kitchen counter without picking up so much as a single speck of dust.

She nodded to her bodyguard, and the burly man removed the cloth from the curator's mouth.

"Please, please, I don't know what you want," the woman begged.

Candice bent forward and stared into Maria Blupoint's eyes.

"It seems I haven't made myself clear. The next words from your mouth had better be the ones I want to hear, or we may have to start cutting instead of breaking."

"Please, please!"

For a second, Candice wondered if the woman really didn't know anything. It was obvious that she was deeply afraid, but not enough. And not of Candice.

"Who gave you the fake crown? And don't make the mistake of asking what crown again."

The woman opened her mouth to say something but thought better of it. She chose to remain silent.

"You are forgetting one thing, Blupoint," Candice said. "Whatever you're afraid of, you should be more afraid of me right now. I'm right here."

Candice nodded at her bodyguard to go ahead, and he pulled out a military-grade combat knife. The curator's eyes widened.

"Wait! He'll kill me. He's already displeased with me," the curator begged.

"Who is he? I won't ask again, and when Trevor here gets started, I won't tell him to stop."

The curator's eyes remained on the knife in Trevor's hand, and then, there it was. Candice could see the moment the curator's shoulders slumped in acceptance of her fate.

"Marco Brambilla rules the city," Maria Blupoint said in a low voice. "I have been bringing him items I felt were worth his time over the years, and he had counterfeits made of the ones he liked."

"So, you found the crown of thorns," Candice surmised.

"Yes. I don't know how he was able to get a forgery, but I decided to sell it to Mr. Lorenzo, as the museum didn't have any record of the crown."

Candice studied the curator for a couple of seconds and nodded in satisfaction. The woman had told her version of the truth as she saw it.

Now she had a name, she didn't need the curator anymore.

"Untie her."

Candice was already heading out of the kitchen when the curator spoke behind her. "Mr. Brambilla isn't easily intimidated, and he is not a forgiving man."

Candice didn't bother stopping as she made her way to the front door.

It looked like Marco Brambilla had the crown of thorns, and Candice would do anything to get her hands on it.

13

"**I** believe we have a problem."

Mark had allowed the group to take the night to rest after the attack on the ranch, but the next morning, he didn't waste any time calling everyone to the sitting room. He sat on the largest sofa with Gen by his side and Lucilius at the other end. Josephine and Isabella sat on the other sofa, while O'Neal was in the armchair.

It was time to get everyone on the same page.

"A minimum of two strike teams attacked the ranch last night, and I believe they will come back because we gave them the option to retreat."

Mark felt Gen go tense beside him. She was the one who had championed their non-lethal approach to the combat of the night before. "That's okay, because you all know that taking a life isn't something we take lightly," he continued gently. "This just means we have to be better prepared for them next time."

O'Neal was the first to respond. "Well, logically, killing our adversaries would make sure they don't have the opportunity to strike at us again, but I stand with Genesis Isherwood. We should be about second chances," he stated bluntly.

Mark saw the rest of the group nod in agreement and relaxed. While Gen could demand that everyone obey her no-killing policy, it was good to see that the rest of the group had that same belief embedded in them.

Well, almost everyone, Mark thought as he saw Lucilius frown from the corner of his eyes.

"So, what's our next step then?" Isabella asked.

"Even though we're agreed on a non-lethal policy regarding humans, it doesn't mean we can't be proactive. We will tighten our defences and see if we can track down those responsible before they come at us again," he informed the group.

"Then we should have followed them last night or taken one for interrogation," Lucilius said sharply.

Mark saw Gen shake her head and open her mouth to reply when he cut in. "In hindsight, I think Lucilius is right. We should have followed the men last night. Perhaps they would have led us to their leader. And maybe we could have gotten information by questioning one of the men. Don't forget, they attacked us with the intention of killing Gen and anyone else that stood in their way."

Mark had chosen not to tail their attackers the night before because he had been worried that a third team could have been waiting to strike from the shadows.

"Does that mean that we wait for them to come at us again?" Josephine asked with a worried look.

"No. I got a good look at the leader of the team. We could ask Theo for help; maybe see if we can meet up with Sergeant Oliver Barbeau," Mark suggested. "He helped us with the sketch artist when we needed a way to find Josephine and O'Neal."

Josephine frowned, and Mark realized she didn't know about the sergeant who had helped them in Saskatoon.

"How will we get to him this time?" Gen asked. "We had to leave in a bit of a hurry, if you remember."

Mark remembered. He and Gen had gone to see the sergeant under the guise that they had information pertaining to the attack on Liam Cuttaham, the then sheriff of Dundurn. The sergeant had become suspicious of them and wanted to know where their information originated from. Mark and Gen had to make a quick escape from the police station to avoid being detained.

"I see your point. Hopefully, Theo will be able to smooth things over. I don't see any other way of finding out who they are," Mark said.

"We have magic," Lucilius stated.

"Magic? What do you mean?" Gen asked.

"If the wizard was here, it would be a simple thing. I'm wondering…if the wizard can do it, maybe someone here can also perform the same feat."

Again, Mark had to admit that Lucilius had a point. He looked around the sitting room at the faces of the people gathered there. Isabella and Lucilius were out of the question, as they didn't have any magical abilities. That left Gen, Theo, Josephine, and himself.

Mark understood the nature of all their abilities, though he had to confess that O'Neal's was a bit confusing.

"I'm not too sure any of us here can do that," Mark said. Lucilius shrugged.

"Mark can," O'Neal said.

"I can?"

"He can?" Gen asked in surprise.

"He senses magic, doesn't he?" O'Neal continued. "All he has to do is stretch out his senses and see if he can detect the people he's after. That's what Myrddin Emrys Wylit would do."

Mark blinked in stunned surprise, his mind racing. Could he do that? How? He knew he could sense magic and people's essence. Up until now, he had considered that ability as a mere offshoot of his fighting prowess. Ever since he'd become able to tap into his ancestors' memories, he had become an unstoppable combat warrior. He hadn't considered that he could also use that ability to sense essence in a different way.

"I think that's an angle worth looking into," Mark said. "We'll also try and get in touch with Theo to see if he can contact Sergeant Oliver."

How difficult is it to see the obvious? O'Neal wondered. He had a firm grip on his wandering mind these days, but he couldn't stop the stray thoughts that slipped through the cracks of the wall he'd formed to keep his sanity in place. He had decided to ignore the potential paths that branched out before him whenever anybody spoke or when he felt he had to provide input. He saw Mark saying something to the rest of the group, but what caught O'Neal's attention was the almost transparent bluish cord wrapped around Mark's right wrist. It extended from his wrist down to the ground, all the way across the sitting room and out the door.

O'Neal cocked his head, unable to resist the allure of this new mystery. He had to find out what was at the other end of the cord. His mind expanded, and he felt another crack appear in the wall that held his abilities in place. The blue cord extended out of the house and into the barn where Mark had his make-shift bedroom. Leaning against the wall in a corner was Mark's sword, which is what the cord led to.

The sword shone so brightly that O'Neal had to avert his mind's eye from the glare of its power. He wondered what would happen if he was bonded to the sword on a soul level like Mark was. The thought branched out into new possibilities, and O'Neal felt a sharp pain pierce his brain. He remembered holding the sword once—before he'd gained his abilities. Even then, he'd known that the sword was extraordinary. He wasn't able to lift the sword, as the bond created by Myrddin and the angel Baraqiel had made it such that it was tied to Mark alone.

O'Neal gazed at the sword, and a million possibilities battled to crystalize within his mind. He could hold the sword now, but he knew such power would only destroy him. He could see what the angel and Myrddin had done. If he wanted to, he could tweak the bond to include his genetic code. There was one just factor he wouldn't be able to circumvent: the sword was made with two of the three nails of power. The depth of the power within that sword was unfathomable, and it would fry his mind in an instant.

As O'Neal forced his attention away from the sword, he felt the weapon's aura turn in his direction. Quickly, he slammed his mind shut. The fraction of a second his mind had felt the aura had left huge furrows in the wall protecting his sanity. He snapped back to the present and saw that he was alone in the sitting room. He didn't know how much time had passed and couldn't hear anyone in the house.

He raised a shaky hand to his temple and winced at the pain in the side of his head.

Some doors were not for him to walk through.

Gen saw O'Neal staring off into the distance and hoped he was okay. Out of everyone in the group that had abilities, O'Neal was the only one whose power had a side effect. She had wondered about it ever since Asmodeus, one of the seven princes of hell, had attacked the town.

At one point, Gen thought that O'Neal's inability to control his powers was a reflection of his doubts when he'd been a doctor. But she knew that couldn't be true; they all had doubts at one time or another.

She still struggled with the concept of being the one that had to gather those who would stand against the dragon in her vision. And Mark had a troubled past that sometimes clouded the way he saw things and the decisions he made. As her protector, the burden of making sure Gen was safe could be overwhelming. Even her granddad had his own inner demons to fight that he'd refused to tell her about. She only knew it had something to do with his past, and if it hadn't been for Asmodeus ambushing them in a warehouse some months back, she wouldn't even have been aware of his troubles.

She'd felt Lucilius's frustration over losing his powers and his immortality. What had been a part of his life for centuries was now gone, and Gen didn't think she could begin to understand the depth of his loss.

Josephine had once confessed that she was worried she would relapse; that the cancer would come back. She had tried to reassure her that the healing was permanent, but there was only so much she could do.

They were all broken people made whole by the grace of the Creator.

Mark dismissed the meeting, and the group made their way out of the sitting room, except for O'Neal. He remained in his chair with that far-off look on his face, and she considered shaking him awake.

"Don't disturb him," Mark said, reading her mind.

"I'm just worried he'll get lost in himself again."

"Yeah, but I heard Josephine say that O'Neal told her it was normal and jolting him out of his trance could be dangerous for him."

Gen sighed, but then she refocused on the reason she'd remained behind after the meeting.

"What about the YouTuber?" she asked Mark.

"Russell Patel?"

"Yes. I still feel he's involved somehow."

"Okay. We definitely need to reach Theo."

"Maybe regarding the soldiers. But Patel's info is on social media. I know where he lives; Isabella found his address."

"So, how do you want to do this? Should we contact Theo first or pay this dirtbag a visit?"

Gen shrugged. "I'm okay with either, or both."

"Then I suggest we pay Russell Patel a visit, then stop at the station to see Theo." Gen nodded. She gave O'Neal one last look as they left the sitting room.

Myrddin didn't sleep well. Surprisingly, the mattress hadn't been too bad, but he just didn't feel right without his powers for such a long period of time. He felt…off.

There were no windows in the room, so he couldn't even be sure what time of day or night it was. It was still just as gloomy as when he was first brought here, and the lone lightbulb hanging from the ceiling didn't help.

Myrddin studied the little room for hours, looking for a way to escape, but there simply wasn't one. Even the door was sturdier than it looked, and his futile attempts to knock it down had done nothing but hurt his shoulder.

He leaned back in the chair and rested his hands on the table. His wrists were raw, the skin torn in several places from rubbing against the manacles. The slightest movement sent a shot of pain through his hands.

He would have been able to heal himself if he could tap into his powers, but the manacles stood in his way like a mountain that was impossible to climb.

Myrddin was angry. Why hadn't he been better prepared? He'd been overconfident, believing that nothing could harm him or pose a problem his powers couldn't handle.

With that confidence came a forgetfulness about everything that had happened in his life. He had come to trust in the "arm of the flesh" and, like he'd read countless times, the "arm of flesh" was usually unsuccessful. It failed because of short-sighted men like Marco, who did what they wanted without consideration for anything but themselves.

Since almost the beginning of time, Myrddin had tried to do what was right. That meant doing as much good as possible, for as many as he could. Meeting men like Marco often made that difficult, but he knew his innate goodness was his strongest magic. He had always found that doing good had the habit of conquering anything that wasn't right. Sure, magic was a useful tool for dealing with evil; but having the right attitude about his gifts was his true power.

In fact, he saw that each member of the group had that same gift. Desiring to do the right thing for the right reasons, no matter the consequences, was the most important feature every member of their team possessed. No evil could or would ever be able to defeat them in their journey, and he was more confident of that now, even in his seemingly hopeless situation. Good will conquer all.

As he considered this realization, he became so grateful that the pain in his wrists suddenly waned. He stopped struggling to release his hands from the manacles and instead kept himself as calm as possible to listen for the "still, small voice."

As the world's greatest magician, he was used to making spectacles like thunder and whirlwinds, but this revelation was very clear.

You need to be quiet and calm to hear the still, small voice.

These revelations opened a floodgate of divine inspiration. He saw the true reality of his situation. It wasn't hopeless. He wasn't beaten. Inspiration and truth flooded his consciousness, and suddenly he knew what needed to be done!

It didn't make sense that obsidian could be forged into metal; it went against the natural order of things.

And, since gold obsidian nullified magic, there was no way magic could have been used to create the handcuffs, either.

Myrddin smiled ruefully. As if opening his eyes for the first time, he saw specks of...gold? He looked intently and saw that a tiny piece of gold obsidian had flaked off the manacles. He felt like screaming for joy. Not only because he had found a way out, but because he had done something he hadn't done for a very long while: he had listened to the still small voice. The most powerful voice there is had told him what to do.

There was no way obsidian could be forged into metal.

Which means...

Myrddin looked around, feverish with new hope.

It must have been painted or sprayed onto the handcuffs!

There was a nail sticking out from the table where he had broken off a piece of the wooden surface earlier. He laughed at the irony of the situation as he rubbed the manacles against the tip of the exposed nail. It was slow going, but he didn't allow his focus to waver. He continued scraping the handcuffs against the nail, ignoring the pain that shot through his hands with every movement. After what felt like an hour, he stopped to inspect them again.

A thin, jagged line had formed along one of the interlinking chains, revealing the rusty red colour of aged iron. Myrddin smiled. One thing about magic was that it was governed by unalterably precise laws. A rune had to be exactly right, a chant's pronunciation faultless, a circle perfectly round and unbroken.

Myrddin poured all his energy into the jagged line and felt the essence build there. He chanted a spell of power, and though faint, it obeyed, and a blade of air appeared hovering over the jagged line. With a whisper, he sent the blade of air slashing down, and the chains connecting the handcuffs broke apart.

Myrddin felt his essence flood back into his spirit as he took a deep breath and looked around the small room with new eyes. The gold obsidian around the villa was still affecting his powers, but the essence he had regained was enough for him to form a disintegrating spell, which he aimed at the wall facing the door. The spell hit the wall and instantly dissolved the cement, plaster, and wood, creating an oval large enough to walk through.

He stepped out of his prison and looked around. He didn't waste any time casting an optical illusion spell to make himself invisible once again. Fortunately, he was too far from the main house where Marco Brambilla was staying for the guard dogs to catch his scent. He cast a levitating spell. This time, he hovered only about six feet above the ground to ensure it wouldn't drain his limited essence. Being so low meant that he could easily be grappled to the ground if he was discovered, but Myrddin had no intention of letting anyone get close to him.

He made a beeline for the compound's exit, flying swiftly across alleys, stopping between every building to sense and listen for guards. Soon, he saw the wall that surrounded the villa looming ahead of him. When he was close, he gathered his remaining energy and created an air spell aimed at the ground beneath his feet. Air shot from his hands and hit the ground, making enough thrust to boost him over the wall.

His essence drained, Myrddin's optical illusion disappeared, and he dropped to the ground on the other side of the wall, laughing with relief as he rolled to break his fall. He was out.

The effects of the gold obsidian did not go beyond the villa's perimeter. He felt whole again. Weak, but whole. He healed his wrists silently, the pain already lessened considerably by the simple power of listening to the divine. He felt invigorated after the ordeal and grateful for the teaching. Even the greatest magician in the world must listen, learn, and practice—each and every day.

What a revelation!

Myrddin looked back at the villa as he walked away, promising himself that he would be back to find the crown of thorns.

14

"**A**re you sure we have the right address?" Gen asked from the passenger seat. Mark took the question as rhetorical and decided not to answer. He had googled the address after finding it on Russell Patel's Facebook page, and while the neighbourhood looked a little dicey, it still had the feel of a community.

Isabella leaned forward from the back seat and looked through the windscreen. Mark could sense that she was uneasy and didn't like where they had ended up.

"What number are we looking for?" he asked to divert their attention from the run-down buildings around them. He stretched out his senses to try and gauge the mood of the residents in the area.

Teenagers who had been swaggering along the sidewalk stopped to leer at the van as it rolled past them. Mark decided to keep an eye, or rather, his senses, locked on them. Just up ahead, he saw a large sign that read '32' staked to what looked like a shed or a tiny storage room.

"Guess we're here," he said as he parked the van next to the curb.

Isabella opened the door and hurried out. Mark sighed. He'd intended for her to wait in the car, but it looked like the plan had changed. Gen was clearly thinking the same; as she stepped out, she gave Isabella a meaningful glance.

"There's no way I'm waiting for you guys in the car," Isabella said flatly. Gen nodded without argument, and Mark took a moment to look around. In addition to the youths they had passed earlier, there were a few passersby on the street.

"We need to do this quickly," Mark said as he walked to the front of the shed-like building.

"Russel Patel?" The building's slight wooden frame rattled and shook as Mark knocked. He sensed a presence within the apartment and heard a sharp intake of breath.

"We are here regarding one of your video podcasts," Mark said in a reassuring tone. There was a sound of shuffling feet and a key turning in the lock. The door opened a crack, and Mark stared at Russell Patel. The man was in his early thirties and had the pallid look of someone that stayed indoors most of the time. Although he was slim and gangly, his posture was simultaneously confrontational and defensive.

"Who are you, and what do you want?" Russell snarled.

Gen felt her spirit become immediately troubled when he spoke. She stepped closer to Mark, allowing Russell Patel to get a better view of her. He sized her up without any hint of recognition before settling on Mark again, so she took that moment to study his soul.

Ever since she'd brought Mark back from the brink of death, her perception of everything around her had changed. She could see people's life forces and even detect when they were lying.

Examining Russel, she saw purple and black colours swirling around his insides. Gen knew she stood before a person filled with bitterness. She didn't know how she knew, but she was certain of the assessment.

"What do you want?" Russell asked again.

"You've been airing a video and calling it a sham," Gen said.

"Look, lady, I make a lot of videos, and I've exposed a lot of shady characters."

"This was recent," Gen said. "It involved the healing of a little girl."

Russell did a double take as he really noticed her for the first time.

"You're the woman from the video," he said.

Gen could now see fear mixed with the swirling colours that permeated the man's soul. He tried to step back and shut the door, but Mark must have sensed his intention because he leaned forward, forcing the fragile door open with his weight. Russell staggered back, and Gen followed Mark into the tiny room. Isabella joined them and shut the door behind her. There was barely enough space for all of them, and Gen was squeezed up against Mark's back. Russell Patel fell back into the only chair in the room and glared at them.

"You must know, I don't scare easily," he said. "I call it as I see it, and people need to know the truth."

Mark snorted at Russell's weak attempt at bravery. It was obvious: Russell was scared out of his wits.

"The truth, you say?" Gen laughed bitterly. "How is inciting your listeners against me telling the truth? Was that your plan from the onset? Who put you up to it? It's obvious you don't have the clout to handle what we've been up against." Gen hadn't intended to lose her cool, but Russell's brazen assumption that he was on the side of justice was irritating. She didn't realize she'd been moving toward him until she saw that he had backed the chair up against the wall, trying to get as far away from her as possible.

"What do you want?"

This time, the question came out as a squeak, and Gen noticed Russell shaking.

"How did you get the video?" Mark asked.

Russell shot fearful glances between Mark and Gen before answering. "I received a mail with a flash drive. It contained the video with a note." Russell scavenged around his desk and produced a crumpled note. He fumbled to smooth it out, but Mark snatched it away and handed it to Gen.

The note consisted of only a short sentence, "Enough with the lies," scribbled in neat handwriting. Gen showed the note to Mark, who shrugged after looking at it.

They had reached a dead end. There was no way Russell Patel could be in on the attack at the ranch, which meant he was only a puppet.

She looked around the tiny room and hid a grimace. The place was stuffy and littered with fast food wraps and plastic spoons.

"It would only be proper to get your facts straight before twisting the truth, or in your case, reporting plain lies," she said as she headed for the door.

"You're saying the video isn't fake?"

Gen heard the mockery in Russell's voice. The weasel was braver now after realizing that he wasn't going to be hurt. She thought of answering him but decided that he wasn't worth the trouble.

"What a cheerful guy," Isabella remarked as they left the shed and headed back down the street.

Before she could reply, Gen noticed a gang of four youths leaning against the van.

Mark had hoped they'd leave without any incident, but it looked like he wouldn't be getting his wish. He studied the four young men gathered around the van waiting for them, already becoming pissed off by their bravado. He was glad they hadn't brought Lucilius along, as this would have ended very badly for the young men.

He lengthened his stride to reach the van ahead of Gen and Isabella. One of the young men—probably the leader—straightened up and tried to stare Mark down. His three friends quickly stepped to his side, also trying their best to look intimidating. The gang leader looked to be in his early twenties, while the youngest member of the group couldn't have been older than fifteen or sixteen. They all looked pretty scrawny, and the fifteen-year-old had some pimples on his forehead.

"Shouldn't you kids be in school or something?"

The gang leader puffed out his chest in what Mark assumed was a pose designed to scare him.

"Before you do something stupid, ask yourselves, is it worth the beatdown?" Mark could tell they'd expected him to be cowed by their numbers and were surprised by his words. The gang leader stepped forward, and Mark shook his head grimly.

"Don't do that, friend. Right now, we can both walk away with our dignity intact. You make a move, and I'll take it you intend to harm me and my friends here. Believe me when I say it won't end nicely for you."

The youths fidgeted. Mark could see the fear in their eyes and hoped they would be reasonable and walk away. For a moment, he thought he wouldn't have to fight them, but then a determined look settled on the gang leader's face.

Mark tensed, about to explode into motion, when he felt Gen's hand on his arm.

"We are sorry for coming into your neighbourhood unannounced," she said. "I know you want to protect the people here, and I can assure you, we mean no harm. We only came to check on someone. That's all."

Gen's words immediately diffused the tension, and the gang leader stepped back.

"Let's go, they're not worth the hassle," one of the youths said. The leader waved his hand around in the air and said, "Hope we don't meet again."

Mark watched the group saunter away and chuckled. "That was quick thinking, Gen," he said as they got back into the van.

"You should have allowed Mark to give them a good spanking," Isabella chided.

"They're just kids," Gen said. Mark smiled internally as he turned the van around and drove off. The gang leader was probably only a year or two younger than Gen, yet she saw them as kids.

He guessed battling demons and immortals gave her a different perspective on life. Unlike others her age, she didn't have the luxury of hanging out with her peers, not giving any thought to who might want her dead.

Mark glanced at Gen as she stared out of the window. She'd had it rough, and he hoped things would get better for all of them.

Marco Brambilla stared at the broken manacles resting on his desk with a mixture of anticipation and awe. They had been in his family for generations, and as far as he knew, no one had ever been able to break free from them. It would seem that there was much more to his intruder than he had thought.

If Marco were anyone else, he might have felt a twinge of fear, but he was Marco Brambilla, son of Edoardo, of the House of Savoy. Marco could trace his lineage back to kings and queens, a fact he was particularly proud of. He had royal blood in his veins.

He had subdued organized crime, and even presidents were subject to his whims.

No! Marco Brambilla feared no one, no matter how great they may seem.

He got to his feet and walked to the bookshelf, reached for a book in the middle of the second row, and tilted it forward. Part of the shelf to his right swung open, revealing a short flight of stairs.

Marco walked down the stairs into a simple room containing a podium with a glass case mounted at its top. He stopped in front of the podium and gazed at the wreath of thorns encased in the glass.

Even with the gold obsidian coating the room's walls and the case, he could feel the power emanating from the relic in the glass case.

Maria Blupoint had stumbled across the crown of thorns during one of her expeditions. The previous owner wasn't aware of the true value of the crown, only saying that it had been in his family for years.

Marco didn't believe in fate, but if he did, he would have said that the crown was made for him to find. One of his numerous companies had financed the expedition, and he was the one Maria had brought the crown to.

Marco always believed he was destined to be a king, and with the power of the crown, the whole world would soon bow before him.

Suspecting that word would get out about the crown, he had quickly arranged to have another forged. Endowing the fake wreath hadn't been easy; it cost the lifeblood of two powerful mages. But it was worth it. The crown he'd given back to Maria Blupoint was indistinguishable from the original.

All things considered, Marco admitted he'd made one single mistake: he'd allowed Maria to live.

The crown's original owner and his entire family met their ends in an unforeseen accident when their country home was swept away by a landslide. The fact that every member of the family was killed in the tragedy hadn't aroused anyone's suspicion.

Once they were taken care of, Marco considered killing Maria, but he valued family, no matter how distant the relation, and he certainly regarded in-laws as members of his family.

Now Maria and her greed had led someone to him. Someone powerful.

Maybe it was time to cut some ties, even if they were blood.

Amy Glover hated having to make this call, but there was no way she could procrastinate any longer. She stared through her study window and watched her six-year-old son play with the family dog. Few things made the boy happy, especially since her divorce, so she allowed him little concessions whenever she could. Although it was getting late, the joy on her son's face made her hesitate to call him in.

With a grimace, Amy turned away from the window and walked to her desk. Unlike her colleagues, who flaunted their achievements and awards, her study was bare, containing only her desk and office chair. On one side of the desk was her computer, and a framed picture of her son sat on the opposite end. Taking a deep breath, she tapped the phone icon on the monitor, and a dial tone disrupted the silence in the study.

The call connected, and Amy saw another study appear on her screen. She was now looking at a desk with a bookshelf behind it. Numerous trophies and plaques adorned the shelf and the wall above it. A man moved into the picture and leaned on the edge of the desk.

"Report."

The statement was made in a calm tone, but Amy wasn't taken in by the man's gentle voice. Dietrich Prince was anything but gentle.

A second of silence reigned as she tried to compose herself.

"I just got word from the sergeant. The mission was unsuccessful."

She had considered calling the mission a failure but quickly changed her mind. Over time, she'd learned that such negative words didn't sit well with Doctor Prince.

"Explain," Dietrich demanded.

Amy studied her boss's face to see if she could decipher his mood. He remained calm on the surface, but she'd also picked up on his tells over the years. Annoyance would flash in his eyes for a fleeting second, and his demeanour would change ever so slightly. Dietrich Prince had a face that Amy might have called ordinary and easily forgettable, but his presence made up for his lack of distinguishing features. He exuded power, and even though it was just a video call, she squirmed in her seat as he glared at her.

"He couldn't determine if the target had the flash drive, and upon engaging, he met with greater resistance than he'd expected." That was as straightforward as Amy could put it.

Patrick Anderson had blabbered to her about super soldiers and invisible shields, but there was no way in hell she'd tell Dietrich that.

"We hired Benedict based on your recommendation, Doctor Glover. It is your mess, so clean it up," Dietrich snapped before terminating the call.

Amy sighed and cursed ever granting Benedict Callaway a favour. The man had been a good analyst, and from the little interaction she'd had with him, he'd seemed focused and determined. Those were the qualities that had convinced her to bring

Doctor Callaway on board. Who would have thought that he'd grow a conscience after three years? Now, here she was, taking the heat for his mistakes.

Amy made another call, and Patrick Anderson's face filled the screen. She could see that she'd called him at an inopportune time as he was trying to wipe the sleep from his face.

"Sergeant Anderson."

"Doctor Glover."

"I cannot reiterate how disappointed I am, Sergeant Anderson. How hard can it be to take down one girl?"

There was a pause while Patrick gritted his teeth with annoyance.

"Like I said, we encountered some complications. We had faulty—"

"I'm really not interested in your excuses. We simply cannot take the chance that she has the flash drive. You need to make this problem go away."

"Understood, Doctor."

"Good."

Amy cut the call and leaned back in her seat. Anderson was good at his job. She'd seen his work firsthand, and he was very useful when it came to quelling dissident voices and getting rid of people that the corporation found unyielding. That was why she was baffled at his failure to complete this simple assignment. Anderson had helped topple third-world governments, yet now he'd come running back with his tail between his legs over one girl.

Just who is Genesis Isherwood?

Amy's thoughts were interrupted as her study door burst open. Her son ran in and gave her a hug, the nanny hurrying in after him, looking apologetic.

"What's up, kiddo? Ready to take your bath?"

Amy waved the elderly woman away and led her son out of the study to his room.

Some things you just have to do yourself.

15

Gen got out of the van the moment Mark parked in front of the sheriff's office. It was still early, at least for Dundurn, and the street was mostly empty. Mrs. Mayfield's shop was still closed, and Morgan Miller was preparing to open his barbershop. Gen waved at him when she saw him look in her direction, and the old man waved back.

She remembered following Theo to Morgan's barbershop when they were kids to get his hair cut. All the kids called him 'Old Miller', and the name stuck. The man didn't seem to have changed much in all the years since. He still walked with a shuffle, and age had increased his stoop a little.

Gen heard the sound of an approaching car and saw Theo drive up and stop in front of the sheriff's office.

"Hey Theo," she greeted as he walked up to her and gave her a quick hug.

"I tried calling you yesterday afternoon," he said. "The strangest thing happened, and it got me worried. I was just about to head to your place but came back to pick up my shotgun."

"What happened?" Mark said from behind Gen. She hadn't heard him walk over, but the tension was apparent in his posture and voice.

Why is he worried?

"Some guy came to town yesterday. He looked suspicious, and with all that's happened, I decided to stop him and demand some I.D."

Theo shifted nervously from one foot to the other, and Gen's heart started pounding. Theo was worried, and Mark must have sensed it.

"Everything seemed okay, and I was just about to let him go when the guy asked me for directions to the ranch."

"The Triple 7?" Gen asked, just to be sure.

"Yeah." Theo nodded.

"What did the man look like?" Mark asked. The intense look on his face kicked Gen's heart rate into an even higher gear.

"About six feet. He looked in shape. Dark hair."

Mark grunted, and Gen knew he wasn't happy with Theo's vague description.

Could it have been the soldiers they'd fought at the ranch? But if it was them, why ask for the address? They already knew where the ranch was.

"How old was he?" Mark asked, and Theo shrugged.

"I couldn't tell for sure, but I'd say about your age or slightly younger. He had the look of a fighter too."

So, not the soldiers, Gen thought. But that didn't help matters. It just meant someone else was also after her.

"The really freaky thing was that I locked the man up with the intention of calling you guys," Theo said. "But I couldn't reach you, so I decided to leave him here for the night."

"So, you still have him?" Mark asked quickly, but Theo shook his head.

"That's where things get weird. When I got to the station this morning...he was gone."

"Gone? What do you mean, gone?"

"The holding cell was open, and he wasn't in there anymore. Gone. I was about to head to the ranch to see if you were okay, but I decided I might need proper backup."

Mark didn't like what he was hearing. The group was suddenly being pursued by multiple enemies. Or was it the work of one foe?

But why come at them from different angles? And was the mastermind behind it the same person who was pulling Russell Patel's strings?

Mark thought he had everything locked down and knew his adversary, but it looked like he'd been kidding himself.

Now Gen's premonition made perfect sense.

"What are you thinking?" Gen asked, and Mark snapped his attention back to the present.

"I'm wondering if Russell Patel's puppet master is the one behind all this."

"Who's Russell Patel? Theo asked.

"The reason we're here, Theo," Gen explained. "We wanted you to look into Russell Patel and also get us in contact with that sketch artist you—"

"What's going on, Gen?" Theo interrupted.

For a second, Gen considered keeping Theo in the dark, but she decided against it. He knew the truth about the group and had been a big help in the past.

"We were attacked by a group…" Gen started.

"Again? Was it…you know?"

"Demons? No, not this time. Just regular folks trying to kill us."

Mark smiled. Trust Gen to try to make light of the dire situation even though any one of them could get hurt—or worse.

"We were attacked yesterday by a group of what we believe to be hired mercenaries," Mark explained. "Russell Patel airs a podcast that's been smearing Gen's image and inciting people against her. And now you've told us of a third party that's after Gen."

Mark watched as Theo's eyes widened in surprise and fear, most likely for Gen's wellbeing.

"We're hoping your friend in Saskatoon can help us sketch one of the attackers and run it through their database," Mark added.

"No can do," Theo said with a shake of his head. "Sergeant Oliver is highly pissed at both of you. He'd probably lock you guys up if you showed your faces around his station."

"Then we'll have to take O'Neal's suggestion into consideration. We need to get ahead of this," Mark said.

What he didn't tell them was that he was very sure that the soldiers would attack again, and next time, the element of surprise wouldn't be on their side.

Candice made sure her makeup was in place as she gazed at her reflection in the small mirror of her powder case. She had been able to track down Marco Brambilla and discovered that he wasn't a mere foot soldier like Lorenzo Lamas. She needed to take a different approach to handling him and hoped an impromptu visit would get the ball rolling.

The car rolled to a stop, and a man who could have passed as Candice's bodyguard's twin walked over. He held a rifle, and she noted three more guards were stationed behind the gate, weapons pointed at the car.

"What do you want?" the guard asked in Italian.

Her sources told her that Brambilla hardly ever left the villa and sent representatives to any function that required his presence. Candice hoped her preparations would be enough. This was the tricky part.

She pressed a button to lower her window and smiled at the guard.

"I'm here to see Marco," she said in English.

"Please, leave. This is private property," the guard said, switching to heavily accented English.

"Tell him my name is Candice Blackburn, and I'm here because we share a common interest in holy artifacts."

If that didn't get the man's attention, Candice was ready to go to phase two—burn everything down.

"Please, turn back and leave. This is private—"

The guard paused and tilted his head to the side, listening to the tell-tale earpiece that every security outfit seemed to enjoy wearing.

Whatever he heard was enough to change his mind. The guard rolled his wrist in the air, and the large gates swung open slowly. Candice relaxed as her bodyguard steered them into the villa.

As soon as they were through the gates, a car drove out from what looked like a bunker and sped to overtake Candice's car. She looked back and saw another car trailing them.

After driving for a few minutes, they reached a large house with several guards stationed out front. The car ahead of them cruised to a stop, and Candice's bodyguard followed suit. As they stepped out of the car, one of the guards stepped toward her with a dog, who sniffed at her briefly before pulling away. The guard nodded to his companions, and one of them gestured for them to go into the house.

The inside of the house was as impressive as the grounds, but Candice restrained herself from looking around. She couldn't appear like a simpleton or someone without class, so she kept her eyes ahead as she followed the guard up a flight of stairs and down a short corridor. He knocked on a door and left, leaving her to wait alone.

Candice smiled inwardly. She knew the game and how to play it. This was a show of power. Marco Brambilla was making sure she knew how unimportant she was.

Luckily, she didn't have to wait long, as the door opened after a minute. A lanky man gave her the once-over and then stepped aside.

Although he smiled, Candice felt like a mouse walking into a lion's den.

Myrddin felt completely revived after a nice shower and a hot meal. His power thrummed within him once more. He flexed his hands and turned them both ways, inspecting the skin. The cuts on his wrists were completely gone, and the powerless feeling had left his soul.

He stood up from the soft mattress he'd spent the day on and stretched. His back popped, and he sighed in contentment. He was good to go, but first, he had to determine what his next step would be.

Was he ready to try and penetrate the villa again, or should he pack it up and head home?

Thinking about home, Myrddin wondered how Gen and the others were faring without him. He assumed everything was okay since neither she nor Mark had called. He wasn't too worried, though; he was sure they could handle anything that came their way. These days, the Triple 7 ranch housed a group of individuals that would make any man tremble—even him.

Gen's powers were growing, and of all the nail bearers Myrddin had known, she was without a doubt the strongest of them all.

Thinking of Gen made Myrddin remember Queen Helena, the mother of Emperor Constantine the Great.

It seemed that stubbornness was a common trait amongst nail bearers, though he was sure Queen Helena would have called it determination.

Myrddin flexed his fingers again. He couldn't leave Europe without finding out whether Marco Brambilla had the crown of thorns or not. But maybe he needed help to face the man again. Myrddin smiled as a name came to mind. It had been years, but he was sure the man would be up for a fight.

Candice walked into the study and stared at the largest man she'd ever seen. He towered over her, her head barely reaching his waist. But his height wasn't what made him so imposing; she detected something else. The man had a presence that scared her, and fear was something Candice had ejected from her soul a long time ago.

She chanted silently, preparing a spell in case things got out of hand, but was utterly surprised when nothing happened.

She looked around in amazement and tried again. It was then that she realized that there was a moment when she'd felt something clamp down on her abilities. She had chalked it up to nerves, but the grin on the face of the giant looming over her told her otherwise.

"Welcome to my abode, said the spider to the fly," Marco said in stuttering English. He grinned again, revealing huge white teeth.

16

G arth was about to do something he hadn't done in a long time: he was going to search for information on the internet. He took a moment to survey his surroundings before getting to work, a habit he picked up in the Citadel. He was sitting in a coffee shop a few streets away from his motel. The coffee was bland, and the waitress was disinterested, but the cafe had one thing going for it: free Wi-Fi.

He sat at the table furthest away from the glass door, keeping his back against the wall. He connected his phone to the internet and googled supernatural phenomena around Saskatoon. Over eight hundred thousand search results came up, and Garth scratched his head in annoyance. He didn't have the time or patience to search through every link. He needed to narrow down the search parameters. He spent the next thirty minutes trying different combinations of search terms, but each search continued to yield a flood of random results.

Shaking his head in annoyance at his technical ineptitude, Garth googled Genesis Isherwood. If Lucilius had them under his control, he could track Lucilius by tailing her, Mark Reynolds, or Melvin Gourdeau.

Genesis's Facebook information popped up, showing her address in Dundurn, Saskatchewan. With a tap, Garth opened the address in his map app, revealing the directions to the Triple 7 ranch. It was all too easy.

It took all of Candice's willpower and self-control to hide her fear. She had to tilt her head back to stare up into Marco Brambilla's grinning face. He hadn't yet introduced himself, but there was no doubt, not with the aura of intimidation that the man was exuding.

Marco walked over to his desk and sat down. Candice was surprised that the leather chair didn't buckle under his weight. The lanky man followed suit and sat on the sofa by the door. Her heart refused to calm down, and the rush of blood to her head was giving her a headache. She tried summoning her essence, but again, she felt nothing. She was cut off from what she'd depended on for more than half of her life, and the feeling of helplessness was unsettling.

"Sit," the big man said, gesturing to the chair in front of his desk. Candice didn't move. She wanted to regain her composure and prove to Brambilla that she wasn't one of his pawns.

After a few seconds, she walked slowly to the offered chair and sat down, crossing her legs and resting her small purse on the desk. She was feeling slightly more in control, and the thudding in her brain grew less intense. As her desire to flee subsided, she realized she hadn't been searched. Was the man before her that conceited, or did he trust the effectiveness of his staff?

"Your men did not search my bag," she said to gauge his response. Marco waved his hand dismissively, a small smile tugging at his mouth.

"You are…how do I say it? Of little importance? I say it right?" Marco looked at the lanky man for confirmation, and the man nodded. He turned back to Candice, grinning. "I try my English when I see American."

Candice fumed, barely hearing Marco as rage overtook fear.

Of little importance!

She tried to reach for her magic again, pouring all her anger into the process. For a second, she felt her fire magic, but it seemed too far away for her to grasp.

"Are all Americans magicians?" Marco's question unsettled Candice, and she lost the will to struggle for her essence.

"What do you mean?" she asked.

"You second...eh...Porca miseria! Perche l'inglese e cosi difficile!"

Candice sat quietly as Marco swore and ranted about his inability to speak English perfectly. She was proficient in more than five languages, including Italian but didn't see the need to tell Marco that. The man had done something to her abilities, and she'd need any advantage she could get.

Again, she felt overwhelmed by the depth of her fear of Marco Brambilla. It would have been easy to become distracted by his polite smiles and goofy disposition, but she knew a hunter when she saw one. She suspected he acted the fool to make his enemies underestimate him.

"Why are you here? You work for the other man?"

He snapped his fingers, and the lanky man hurried over. Marco handed the man some chains, and he grunted as he carried them back to the sofa and sat down again.

Candice felt her heartbeat spike again. She didn't have anything she could use to defend herself against the giant of a man. And what had he meant by his last question?

"Work for who?" she asked.

"The other man...slim...magic user like you, but much, much stronger."

Candice wasn't surprised that Marco knew about her powers; after all, he had incapacitated her essence somehow and cut off her magic.

There was so much she didn't understand, so she decided to gamble and see if she could survive the encounter.

"You have cut off my...magic. How did you do that?" She felt there was no harm in asking, and Marco seemed to relish showing off his control of the situation.

"Family secret," Marco replied. He pulled out a drawer, and Candice felt her body tense up. She relaxed a bit when she saw Marco bring out a cigar. He cut off the end and licked around the exposed end, then lit it, never breaking his stare.

"So, you know other man?" Marco asked as he pulled on the cigar and inhaled deeply. After a brief pause, he exhaled, smoke billowing from his mouth into the air.

Candice considered ignoring his question, but she wasn't sure how far she could push him. She had a feeling that goading him was not a safe option. She was powerless, and it was highly unlikely that her charms would work here.

"I don't know who you're talking about. I work alone," she said.

Marco watched her with a predatory gaze, all the humour now gone from his face. Candice shivered as his eyes locked onto hers.

"You tell the truth. So, why come here? And what do you know about crown of thorns?"

"I don't know anything about a crown—"

"Please, now you lie. Next lie, I break your finger. Next lie, your hand. Understand?"

His words weighed down her shoulders like a sack of rocks. She felt herself nodding and realized just how much trouble she was in.

"I understand. I came here because Maria Blupoint gave me—"

Marco raised a hand. He looked at the lanky man and rattled off some instructions in Italian. Candice did her best to control her emotions, trying to hide the fact that she understood his words. He had ordered the lanky man to take some men and, if she had heard him correctly, put Maria with the fishes. Then he told the man to create a fund for Maria's younger siblings and relations.

"You were saying?" Marco turned back to Candice.

"Maria pointed me in your direction and, since we share a common goal, I decided to pay you a visit," she started. It was only when she saw the satisfied grin on Marco's face that she realized his question had been in Italian.

"I have come to this position not because of my size, Miss Blackburn, but because people underestimate me. What could you offer me that I can't get myself?"

Candice was in a precarious position. She sensed that her fate would be determined by the next words to came out of her mouth, so she considered them carefully.

She had nothing to offer Marco, and her plan of meeting with him as an equal had failed dismally. He would certainly kill her if he felt she was playing him or had nothing to offer. Knowing her life was on the line, Candice played her trump card.

"I know where the greatest wizard that ever lived is hiding. I know how you can get Merlin the Great."

The grin on Marco's face widened as her words sunk in, and Candice felt relief wash through her.

Myrddin took a sip from his cold beer and turned to watch the door. The New Jerry was a small establishment with just enough patrons to keep it going. Presently, the patronage consisted of a couple of people who Myrddin felt should have been making better use of their time. Not that he could judge, seeing as he was also here drinking in the afternoon.

The bar door opened, and a short, stocky man walked in. He was a little over four feet tall, with thick eyebrows and a pudgy nose. Not much to look at, but Myrddin knew he was a force to be reckoned with.

"Myrddin Wylit!" the stocky man bellowed, grabbing him in a strong hug.

"Good to see you too, Trosdan," Myrddin said as he returned the hug and gestured for Trosdan to take a seat.

"What brings you to this part of the world, my friend?" Trosdan asked in a gentle voice as he made himself comfortable on a barstool.

"I'm in a bit of a situation, and I need help."

"What kind of help?"

"I think I've come across the crown of thorns, my friend." Myrddin saw Trosdan's eyes widen.

"Can it be true?"

He grinned and nodded.

After Queen Helena found the three nails of power, Myrddin had deemed it prudent to collect all the objects that had come into contact with Jesus's blood. As part of his ongoing quest to find the relics that came with the resurrection of Jesus the Christ, he had once joined forces with Trosdan to find the Shroud of Turin, the linen cloth that had been wrapped around the body of Christ after the crucifixion.

The authentic Shroud of Turin was now in a secure location known only to the two of them. The last of the three nails of power was with Gen, and all the wood from the cross of the crucifixion had been burnt, the ashes also locked away safely.

Only the crown of thorns had eluded Myrddin. Centuries ago, he'd heard rumours of it being in Palestine, but it was just a trap laid by the accursed. Trosdan's intervention had saved his life. Trosdan was after the crown, but for personal reasons.

"Where is the crown?"

The question snapped Myrddin back to the present.

"I believe Marco Brambilla has it."

Trosdan grunted at the name.

"You 've heard of him?"

"Who hasn't? Nasty fellow, that Brambilla. His family line can be traced back to the last kings and queens of Italy. Rumour has it that the government is in his pocket, but I don't know how true that is. If he has the crown, it could spell trouble."

Myrddin couldn't agree more. He recounted his experience at the Brambilla Villa.

"You couldn't use your magic?" Trosdan asked in disbelief when Myrddin finished.

"No. It seems the legends about gold obsidian are true."

"You've seen this with your own eyes?" Trosdan insisted.

"I was handcuffed in it! It rendered me completely powerless."

"So, that's why you need my help," Trosdan said thoughtfully.

Myrddin nodded and watched his old friend. They had been through so much together, but he hadn't seen Trosdan for years. People change over time—and some, not for the better.

He needed Trosdan because he had one very unique ability: magic didn't work on him. He was one of the few living human beings that was created that way. Myrddin liked to call them Zeros. Trosdan made for the perfect assassin, as no magical trap or spell could harm him. He couldn't be detected by any locator spell, and to him, magical items were just ordinary objects.

Despite the accursed's attempts to wipe them out, Trosdan's kind had provided the balance the world needed during Myrddin's time, and it seemed like he needed his help once again.

Trosdan looked up at Myrddin with a mischievous glint in his eyes and a smile on his face.

"When do we do this?"

Patrick didn't believe in failure. Like his mother always told him, "Try and try again." So, he was going to try again. Only, this time, he was better prepared and knew the kind of forces he would be up against. He didn't know what Genesis Isherwood and Mark Reynolds were, but he believed any war could be won with superior firepower.

Patrick picked up the AA12 Atchisson Assault Shotgun from the motel bed and snapped the chamber in place. The modified shotgun had a better recoil than the average shotgun. It had greater firepower and was able to shoot explosives with a very high level of accuracy. Patrick looked around at his team. They all had grim looks on their faces as they prepared the various types of high-powered assault weapons they held.

If a bat doesn't do the job, bring a freaking sledgehammer to the fight, Patrick thought as he watched Carter pick up an XM2010 Enhanced Sniper Rifle. Patrick's smile was grim and dangerous as he thought of the damage they would unleash on the occupants of the Triple 7 ranch.

17

CONSTANTINOPLE, 327 A.D.

Calisto stilled his breathing as the plump cult member ran for his life, the patter of his feet on the pavement echoing loudly through the late night. He watched from behind a building as the man stopped in front of a tavern. The cult member was wheezing and gripping his knees as he took in huge gulps of air.

The man was difficult to find but easy to follow. Even though cult members had been popping up like termites from a rotten tree, arresting them had yielded nothing.

Calisto peered closely at the tavern. The crooked sign that dangled from the wooden post out front bore the inscription 'The Whispering Owl.' The cult member looked around nervously, not spotting Calisto.

Earlier that night, Calisto and the city guard had raided another hideout after an informant told them of suspicious late-night activities taking place.

There were five cult members in the dirty room, and when one of them ran out the back door, Calisto had stopped the city guard from chasing after the man. He knew from experience that they wouldn't get much information from the cult members, as they were very loyal to their leader and didn't seem to fear pain or torture. The cultists seemed ready to die rather than betray their brotherhood.

Trailing the chubby man had been easy. Now, Calisto would see who the cult member was going to meet up with. The night breeze caressed his cheeks as he watched the cultist banging his fist on the tavern door.

A moment later, the door swung open, and the man hurried inside. Calisto watched patiently as a brawny, thick-armed man glanced up and down the street before moving back to shut the door.

Then he made his move.

He closed the distance between his hiding spot and the tavern in a matter of seconds, and before the door could shut, he kicked it in. It slammed into the brawny man, who staggered back as Calisto pushed his way into the tavern. From the corner of his eyes, he saw the cult member scrambling to get out of the seat he had just taken, but he was too slow. Calisto rushed in and punched him in the face.

He needed the man alive.

The cultist's heavy frame slammed onto the floor,

blood spraying from his broken nose. Calisto heard a sound behind him and ducked to the side. The air next to his ear stirred as the thick-armed man swung a cudgel at his head, missing him by mere inches. The motion exposed the man's neck, and Calisto didn't waste his chance. He jabbed at the man's throat with his fist and watched as he seized up and dropped the cudgel. Calisto knocked the man out with a final punch to the side of the head.

The tavern was now quiet, except for the sound of the chubby cult member groaning in pain as he struggled to his feet.

"Just the two of us now," Calisto smiled.

"Wait, please, I don't know anything," the cult member pleaded.

"That will be for me to decide," Calisto said. "I am looking for a wizard called Derog the Banished. He is your leader, and you will take me to him."

"I do not know who this...Derog is. Please don't hurt me."

Calisto frowned. The man had to be lying, yet the words coming out of the cult member's mouth sounded sincere.

"You are a member of the group that serves Derog. You and your fellow cultists desire to cause chaos and overthrow the government."

"No, no, no!" the cult member replied. "I desire none of these things. I only wish to provide for my family. Someone approached me. He said I should gather at a certain place every day. The man pays handsomely for us to gather. That is all I know."

The man was telling the truth. Calisto could hear it in his voice.

"Who hired you?"

"That would be me," a voice rang out from the shadows.

Calisto spun around, his short sword ringing as he drew it from its sheath. He chastised himself for being so careless and not checking the tavern for other lifeforms. He hadn't heard the movement behind him, but he recognized the voice.

The accursed stood before him.

Lucilius was leaning casually against the wall, a bored expression on his face. Remus and Atticus stood on either side of the tavern door. The voice belonged to Marius, who now smiled and walked toward Calisto.

"I employed the poor fool trembling before you," Marius said.

He stopped a few feet in front of Calisto, the smile on his face twisting into a sneer as hate filled his eyes.

"CUT YOUR THROAT."

The words hit Calisto like an avalanche. He felt the sword tremble in his hands as he considered obeying the command. The words swirled in his mind as he struggled to resist the imperative to end his own life.

He fought the urge, then smiled as he shrugged off the command and stood his ground. Gripping the pommel of his sword, he prepared to fight. It would be a fight that he couldn't win, but maybe he could take down one of the accursed before he died.

"I did what you wanted," the cult member told Marius, the fear still oozing out of him.

"You did well," Marius assured the man. Calisto stood poised and ready to spring into action, but still. If the accursed wanted to talk, he was willing to delay the inevitable. It might give him time to think of a way out of his dilemma.

"Can...can I go?" The cult member looked at Calisto, then turned fearfully back to Marius.

"Don't worry about him. You are free to go," Marius said with a shooing motion. The cult member breathed a sigh of relief as he hurried to the door.

"Wait. Just one more thing." Marius continued smiling as the cult member looked at him expectantly.

"Stop breathing." The words were said softly, without the anger and rage that Marius had thrown at Calisto earlier. Calisto watched as the cult member looked confused for a few seconds before falling to his knees, clutching his throat. He opened his mouth as he tried to draw in as much air as he could, but Calisto knew it was a wasted effort.

The man's fate was sealed. Marius clapped his hands gleefully as he watched the cult member writhing in agony on the floor.

Calisto used that moment to make his move. He rushed at Marius, hoping to cut him down while he was distracted by the dying cult member.

He had only taken a few steps when an unseen force slammed into him and threw him across the tavern. He hit the wall and slumped to the ground. It took a moment to recover his wits, and he remained on the floor with his back against the wall. Judging from the ringing in his ears and the way the room was swimming in front of his eyes, he suspected he might have a slight concussion. Calisto raised his hand and was glad to see that his sword was still in his grip. Muscle memory from countless years of training and fighting had taught him to never let go of his weapon. He struggled to his feet and glanced at Atticus, ignoring the agonizing pain in his back.

"You'll have to do better than that," Calisto said with a grin.

His plan remained the same; he hoped to take out one of the accursed. Of the four of them, he believed Marius was the most dangerous. Marius could control anyone with his words of power, which meant he could turn anyone into his puppet. Calisto had experienced the grip of his power, and it was terrifying. Only his loyalty to Queen Helena made it possible for him to break free from Marius's will.

So, he had to kill Marius. As long as the accursed was alive, Queen Helena would have to look over her shoulder for all the remaining days of her life.

Calisto couldn't have that.

He struggled to his knees and slowly slipped out a dagger strapped to his ankle. He would need to be quick for his plan to work.

"Why do we waste our time with him? Kill him and let's get out of here," Remus said with a dismissive wave.

Calisto gauged the distance between him and

Marius as he got to his feet. One thing he'd come to realize about the accursed was that they relished showing their superiority. They would give him time to recover, believing there was nothing he could do.

Calisto feinted to his right while flinging the dagger in his left hand at Atticus. Marius gave a yelp of surprise and stumbled back in fear. Calisto gripped his sword tightly and took the opportunity to rush at Marius. As he ran, Remus drew a bow from thin air, an arrow appearing in his other hand.

Meanwhile, Atticus blasted the dagger out of the way, and Lucilius grinned wolfishly at Calisto as he prepared to intercept his attack.

Calisto saw his death approaching, but he was content. Marius was within his reach. With all his might, he swung his sword at the accursed's neck. Calisto heard the twang of Remus's bow as an arrow shot toward him. Atticus was frantically preparing another spell, but Calisto knew they were too late.

Marius would die tonight.

Remus's arrow struck the blade of Calisto's sword and fell away uselessly. His killing blow cut into Marius's neck, and the accursed fell backward.

Calisto pressed home his advantage. He spun, preparing another blow, but Lucilius had reached the fight. He parried the strike, and Calisto now had to focus all his attention on the sword master.

They exchanged rapid strikes, and Lucilius's sword sliced into his arm, leaving a thin cut. Lucilius lunged forward, but Calisto sidestepped the attack with sure feet.

He knew he wouldn't be able to take on the remaining three immortals at once, so he kept Lucilius in front of him, blocking Atticus and Remus's line of sight. Immobile and bleeding heavily from the wound in his neck, Marius was done fighting for now.

Lucilius's arm flashed again and again, but Calisto kept blocking the accursed's attacks. He took his chance when he saw an opening, ducking below a wild swing. Now closer to Marius, Calisto moved in to finish off the wounded immortal.

But before he could reach his target, Calisto felt fresh pain blossom in his thigh as one of Remus's arrows pierced his flesh, bringing him to his knees a few feet from Marius.

The opening had been a trap.

He started crawling toward Marius when, suddenly, he felt a force envelop him. He was lifted off the ground and left hovering helplessly mid-air as the remaining accursed gathered around him.

"You could have warned me that I was bait!" Marius yelled with annoyance.

"And spoil the fun?" Remus replied.

"Where's the fun in almost having your head lopped off?" Marius clutched at his bleeding neck.

"You should have seen that coming," Lucilius said, not bothering to hide his condescension.

"Not all of us enjoy fighting like animals," Marius snapped.

"And that's why I remain untouchable," Lucilius answered.

Marius raised an eyebrow and pointedly looked at Lucilius's wounded eye with an expression that said, "Untouchable, my foot."

The cut above Lucilius's eye, a gift from the nail bearer who had struck him with one of the three nails of power, had refused to heal and was turning milky white.

"What do we do with him?" Atticus asked, nodding toward Calisto's floating form. Not one to ever give up, Calisto was still struggling to move his body, but Atticus's magic was too strong.

"Kill him. He's a pain," Marius stated flatly.

Atticus nodded in agreement and stretched out his hand to Calisto, who moaned as the bubble holding him in place contracted.

"Wait!"

Marius gingerly rubbed his neck. The wound had healed, but his throat still felt sore. A thin scar marred his skin where Calisto's sword had struck.

"Let him live and see the end. Let him know he has failed when we bring back the queen's head. Let him wallow in his failure. Then we can kill him."

Calisto tried to move again, but his efforts were futile. He silently cursed his folly and the accursed standing before him.

Remus's face began to ripple, the muscles bulging and twisting as his features reshaped. Calisto stared in dismay as he saw a replica of himself grinning back at him.

"Now you know what we intend to do," Marius said quietly.

"Your queen will die thinking her faithful lap dog killed her."

You will never get close enough, Calisto railed silently.

"I think he wants to say something," Remus laughed.

Calisto pushed against the force containing him, but it was like trying to push away a mountain.

Banishing a higher demon can be a real pain, Merlin thought as he traced a circle of light on Queen Helena's bedroom floor.

The demon had attacked Queen Helena twice now, and Merlin was getting tired of its hit-and-run tactics. The higher demons were more intelligent than their lower kindred.

Merlin knew the demon would attack again, and, this time, he'd be ready. He completed the circle of light and stepped outside of it, chanting as he poured his essence into the spell. The circle blazed brilliantly with power before fading away.

Queen Helena stood by her bed, stoic and determined to play her part. The bags under her eyes were the only clue that she hadn't slept for three days.

"Are you ready for this?" Merlin asked.

"You're certain this will draw the beast here?"

Helena trusted Merlin, but after having been harassed by the invisible entity for three days, she needed some reassurance. She longed for one night of sleep without worrying it would be her last.

"Without a doubt," Merlin replied.

"And I'll be safe within the circle?"

"Nothing inhuman can cross the light."

She gathered the hem of her nightdress and entered the circle, feeling a soothing caress wash over her as she stopped in its center.

"What now?"

"Now we wait. I have projected your aura to make sure the demon senses you. It won't be able to resist."

Helena nodded as she brought out the foot nail from the hidden pocket hemmed into her dress, taking comfort in its warmth. She glanced at the door, expecting Calisto to come in.

"He had to look into an important matter, or he would have been here," Merlin said, reading her thoughtful look.

"I know. I'd just feel—"

"Safer. That's the job of a protector."

"It's more than that. He's more than that."

Merlin felt a shift in the essence surrounding the palace and put a finger to his lips.

The demon was close.

Queen Helena clutched the nail tighter and waited, trying to calm her beating heart. She had put her life in Merlin's hands, and it would be forfeit if his spell didn't work.

Merlin stepped into the shadows created by the lamp on the desk and waited.

A light breeze lifted the bedsheet, and Helena tensed up. They weren't alone. She couldn't see it, but the nail in her palm grew warmer, and she felt the hair on the nape of her neck stand up.

The demon struck swiftly, given away only by the sudden flare of the circle of light. The flash outlined the demon as it sought to break through the barrier. Queen Helena stumbled back but made sure she didn't step out of the perimeter. Merlin was adamant about that rule; she would be safe as long as she remained within the circle.

Merlin whispered a chant, and another barrier sprang up, enclosing himself, Helena, and the demon.

The beast turned fiery eyes in his direction and rushed at the wizard. Helena shouted a warning as its sharp claws raked at him, but the shield surrounding the wizard's body protected him. Merlin continued his quiet chanting. He needed a spell strong enough to drive the denizen of hell back to its habitat.

Merlin ignored the thudding sounds of the demon's blows on his shield. He needed to concentrate on the incantation. The slightest mispronunciation or inaccurate gesture could interfere with the spell, and, while not harmful to Merlin, it could easily provide the demon with an opening to escape.

Wind gathered around him, gradually increasing in velocity and creating a vortex. The demon screeched and tried to escape, but it slammed into the barrier again. It could sense its impending doom and sought to escape its fate.

The vortex grew in power and began to pull at the demon. It tried to resist, digging its clawed feet into the floor.

With a flick of his hand, Merlin shot a beam of light at the demon. The shot unbalanced it, and it bellowed in rage as the vortex sucked it from the physical plane.

It was gone.

A calm settled over the room as the spell expired and the wind died down.

"Is it over?" Queen Helena asked.

"It is."

Helena waited a moment to be sure, then stepped out of the circle of light. Merlin raised an eyebrow at her for doubting him but didn't say anything. The room was in disarray, the bedsheets dishevelled on the floor. Helena sat down on the bed with a sigh of relief.

"Have you found out who was behind this attack?" Helena asked, rubbing her eyes.

"In a way. That's one of the reasons Calisto isn't here. We need to confirm my suspicions."

"And you 're sure it's not the accursed?"

"Reasonably sure. Unless they've decided to change how they operate. The accursed would make it personal; they would attack themselves and not give the...eh, glory, to someone else."

"Maybe they decided to change tactics since they've failed too many times," Helena suggested.

"There is that, but my gut tells me we're dealing with a different player."

"This Derog you mentioned? Your former disciple."

"That is my bet."

What Merlin didn't understand was how Derog could have gotten his ability to cast spells back. A shattered core was irreversible, or so Merlin thought.

How had Derog done the impossible?

18

Mark needed to come up with a plan. Sat around him in the living room, he could see the apprehension on everyone's faces and knew they already suspected what he had to say.

"Okay, I'm not gonna beat around the bush," he said, not wasting any time with niceties. "We'll most likely be attacked soon." He looked around to see how the rest of the group was taking the news. He'd told Gen earlier, and Lucilius already suspected as much. Isabella looked worried, and Josephine had an excited look on her face that Mark found disturbing. As for O'Neal, he looked...well, O'Neal looked like O'Neal.

"How certain are you?" Isabella asked.

"Very certain. About ninety percent sure. A team like that won't back away."

"So, what do we do?" This time, the question came from Gen.

"Be prepared. That's the only thing we can do. It would have been good to find out why they were after Gen, but since that's not an option, we have to stick to surviving."

"But this time, we know they are coming," Lucilius said with a determined look.

"Yes, but they also know that we'll be prepared," Mark replied.

"Now I'm confused," Josephine said. "They know we know that they know?"

Mark nodded as he tried to explain.

"We've lost the element of surprise, as have they. In such a situation, the only thing left to do is proceed and crush the opposition with overwhelming force."

"The protector speaks sense," Lucilius agreed.

"And the question remains, what do we do?" Isabella asked.

"We prepare," Mark said simply. "The containment field is still active, so that's a plus. We can't take the fight to them, but we have the home advantage. We'll use that as much as we can."

"I'm not sitting this one out." Josephine folded her arms across her chest and glared at Mark.

"I agree. We'll need everyone on this one." If his suspicions were correct, the strike team would try to attack them with enough firepower to compensate for their disadvantage. They had seen Mark and Gen's abilities and would try to negate them somehow. At least they still had Josephine and O'Neal as aces in the hole.

Myrddin stared at the wall encircling the Brambilla villa and took a deep breath. He could already feel the gold obsidian suppressing his essence, but now that he knew what to look out for, he believed he could monitor the rate at which his magic was being blocked. He had thought of entering through the front gate, as he figured Marco already knew he was nearby but decided against that option. Why make it difficult for himself?

He cast his air spell and felt his body lift from the ground, struggling for a moment to carry his weight but managing to rise above the villa wall. Releasing the optical illusion spell, he faded from sight. Myrddin flew over the guards and their dogs, taking the same route as the first time. He stopped at regular intervals to recover from his throbbing head and the strain of casting his spell with the gold obsidian nearby.

Arriving at the main house, Myrddin decided that the study would be the best place to start his search for the crown of thorns.

When he reached the balcony, he heard footsteps approaching, and a team of six guards emerged to survey the surrounding area, their guns at the ready. It was obvious they hadn't spotted Myrddin, but they were clearly expecting him. He heard heavy footsteps and sensed Marco approaching.

"Must we go through this again, Wizard?" Marco said in Italian. "I know you are here, even if I can't see you. My men will open fire if you don't reveal yourself."

Myrddin weighed his options. After a brief pause, he released the invisibility spell and raised his hands.

"We have some unfinished business to discuss," Myrddin said in Italian.

Marco tilted his head to the side and studied Myrddin thoughtfully.

"You are either very brave or very stupid, Magician. I will find out which. But before that, I want you to meet someone."

Myrddin frowned and heard someone else approaching. Judging from the light footsteps, he guessed it was a woman. Sure enough, a few moments later, the petite blonde from the auction stepped out onto the balcony.

She stopped by Marco's side and stared at Myrddin. Then, without any warning, she screamed and rushed at him.

Marco told Candice he was expecting an unwanted guest and asked her to follow him to the balcony. It was more of a command than a request, but Candice was curious and, after their earlier discussion, relieved that she had been elevated from prospective fish food to a guest being treated with some measure of civility.

She followed him up the stairs and into what looked like a guest bedroom, the bodyguards running ahead to swarm the balcony.

Marco went outside to speak to the visitor. Waiting in the room, she couldn't overhear their discussion, but when Marco beckoned for her to step forward, she spotted the unwanted visitor for the first time.

Rooted to the spot in shock, Candice stared at Merlin, the greatest wizard of all time. The one responsible for all the pain her family had endured. She didn't realize that the scream she was hearing came from her lips or that she'd crossed the distance and tried to grab Merlin by his neck.

What is he doing here?

Candice tried to channel any essence she could to burn the bastard to the ground, but nothing materialized. Her magic was still blocked. Marco had explained that it had to do with a kind of rock within the building's walls. She was fuming. Of all the moments to be powerless!

One of the guards pulled her away from Myrddin, and she struggled against his grip.

"Enough!" Marco's voice boomed, penetrating her enraged mind, and Candice stopped struggling. "I take it there is bad blood between the two of you."

Bad blood? That was putting it mildly.

"He destroyed my family!" Candice shouted. "Just because he had the power to do so! Well, not anymore."

She glared at Myrddin with hate, and Marco smiled.

Myrddin couldn't understand why the blonde woman had tried to attack him. He didn't recognize her from anywhere other than the auction house. In his surprise and desire to defend himself, he almost revealed that he still had some magic left. His essence was depleting quickly, but he'd meditated before setting out this time and had filled his inner core to the brim. Moving through the air under the illusion spell had drained more than half of his essence and standing on the balcony so near to the gold obsidian reduced it to almost nothing.

"I take it there is bad blood between the two of you."

Surely he would remember her if they'd met before? When they met in Lorenzo Lama's office, he was in disguise, explaining why she hadn't reacted so violently then.

"Sorry to say, Marco, but I don't know this woman." Myrddin shrugged his shoulders.

"It's him. It's Merlin. The one I told you about."

Her words brought a change to the atmosphere on the balcony. Marco's jovial expression changed into that of a cold, calculated killer. The transformation was swift, and the men surrounding them shifted uncomfortably as they sensed their boss's dangerous mood.

"Is that so?" Marco said quietly. "That would explain a lot: how you had endless power; how you were able to break my manacles. Did you know those chains have been in my family for generations? In all that time, not so much as a scratch marred their surface, yet you managed to break them."

Myrddin didn't think Marco's statement deserved a reply, so he merely shrugged. Clearly not appreciative of the wizard's attitude, for a moment, it looked like Marco would strike him. Myrddin wasn't sure he'd survive a punch from the huge man, so he started casting a shield around himself. It would cost him the remaining essence he had, but he had no choice. Luckily, Marco restrained himself, and the plastic smile soon returned to his face.

"Why are you here, Wizard?" Marco asked instead.

"I came for the crown of thorns. I know you have it."

Myrddin noted Marco didn't deny this and also noticed the confused look on the blonde woman's face—she was after the crown as well.

"He has the real crown. I'm sure he didn't tell you that." Myrddin directed his words at the woman, hoping to get her on his side.

"Yes, I have the crown. It is in a safe place," Marco admitted, stepping closer to Myrddin and cupping his chin in a vice grip.

"You don't look like much, Great Wizard. Let us stop this game of posturing. Do you have the nails of power?"

Marco's question elicited a gasp from the blonde woman, and Myrddin knew he'd found a way to sow discord between the two of them.

"I'm not sure what you are asking me, Marco. The nails of—"

Myrddin's words were interrupted by a blaring alarm, and he saw Marco's face twist in anger.

It was the perfect plan.

Myrddin would act as the distraction while Trosdan went looking for the crown of thorns.

Trosdan was worried that Myrddin had laid it on a bit thick outside the walls of the villa. It was all staged for the benefit of the security cameras, but, still, he had found it hard to watch the wizard's performance as he prepared his levitation spell.

He waited for Myrddin to disappear from sight before going south and climbing the wall there. Scaling the high wall hadn't been too difficult, despite his stature and height. Unlike Myrddin, Trosdan didn't shun technology and having custom-made, water-powered suction clamps made it a piece of cake. Trosdan had devised the clamps himself after seeing a larger-scale prototype online, developed by a university in Asia, and tinkering with the design.

Spirals of electric fencing covered the top of the wall, so Trosdan stopped, grunting as his arms shook under the strain. He only had clamps for his hands, meaning his upper body had to do all the work. Using them to get over a much higher building would have been daunting, but, luckily, the villa wall was only about thirty feet high.

The electric wires buzzed ominously, and Trosdan sighed. This part of the plan would be very painful, but again, not impossible.

His genetic mutation not only rendered him immune to magic but also made his skin tough and resilient. Medical science labeled the "condition" scleroderma, but he knew better. His hardened skin was a unique genetic trait in his family that had surfaced across generations.

Trosdan took a deep breath and took hold of the wires of the electric fence. He grunted in pain as close to ten thousand volts surged through his body and launched his body up and over the wires, reaching out with the clamps mid-air and latching back onto the wall on the other side. From here, it was simply a matter of shimmying down.

Safely back on the ground, Trosdan took a deep breath and removed the clamps from his hands.

It seemed Myrddin's distraction succeeded in drawing most of the guards away; he had no trouble running from building to building, avoiding the few guards remaining around the perimeter.

When he arrived at the main house at the center of the villa, he used the suction clamps again to climb up to an open window one level below the balcony. Myrddin had explained the layout of the house, so Trosdan knew where to find the study. He gently dropped down into a dark, empty corridor. He could hear the commotion down the hall as guards swarmed up the stairs, brandishing assault rifles and a variety of other weapons. Staying low,

Trosdan quickly made his way to the study. Glancing both ways to be sure he hadn't been spotted, he opened the door and silently slipped in.

Everything was as Myrddin had described it. Everything, that was, except for the slim man staring at him in surprise. Silence reigned for a couple of seconds as they looked at each other in shock. The man recovered first and jumped to his feet, his hand going for the gun in his shoulder holster.

Trosdan swore as he rushed at the man, slamming into him with his full weight and tackling him to the floor. The man doubled over in agony, and Trosdan used the opportunity to slam a well-aimed fist into the side of the man's head.

The man passed out with a final groan, and Trosdan got to his feet.

He looked around the study. He needed to be quick. He didn't know what was happening upstairs, but he could hear loud voices.

Myrddin told him that when he had been in the study, he unleashed his power in a bid to overcome the gold obsidian suppressing his power. He was unsuccessful but had noticed a surprising fact. For the microsecond his power was active, the room glowed with essence, and Myrddin saw a cluster of fingerprints imprinted on the books in the middle row of the bookshelf.

Trosdan moved swiftly to the bookshelf and began to prod and push at the books. One didn't budge when he tried to push it aside. Smiling, he tilted it toward him, and a section of the shelf swung open. He suppressed the urge to yell out in triumph as he walked down the stairs that appeared in front of him.

At the bottom was a small room, and at its center stood a podium supporting a glass case. Even though Trosdan couldn't sense magic, he knew that what was inside the glass case was special, as it emitted a feeling he couldn't quite describe. He walked to the podium with a feeling of awe when an alarm started blaring, and the hiss of gas filled the room.

19

G arth didn't know how prepared one had to be to fight one of the horsemen of the apocalypse, so he erred on the side of caution. He felt restored, and his ring was bursting with stored essence as backup. When he'd escaped the police cell in that town that time seemed to have forgotten, it was the ring that provided enough essence for his invisibility spell.

He went back to his motel and rested, using the time to restore his spent energy and recharge the ring to its maximum power.

Now he was ready.

It was dark when he parked his rental car on the side of the highway. His plan was to approach on foot rather than roll up to the front door and announce his presence. He couldn't just cruise into the lion's den and hope he'd be invited for dinner.

Garth got out of the car and quietly headed down the path to the ranch, his black pants and jacket blending in well with the darkness. Magic could render such precautions useless, but based on all the research the Citadel had done on the four horsemen, Lucilius was as normal as they came when magic was involved. Not that he was the weakest target; on the contrary, reports stated that Lucilius was the strongest of the horsemen and their leader. Garth was still baffled as to why Lucilius had decided to make the Triple 7 ranch his base. It was in the middle of nowhere, in an area that was still under development. And why was he separated from the rest of the horsemen? From the information the Citadel had gathered over the centuries, Garth understood that the four horsemen always moved together. Had there been a falling out amongst them? Garth hoped that was the case, as it would make it possible to pick them off one by one. Together, the four horsemen were undefeatable, which was why he couldn't understand why the Citadel wasn't jumping at the opportunity to remove one of them from the picture.

He shook off the thoughts spreading through his mind as the entrance of the Triple 7 ranch came into view. He needed to be focused to get the job done.

Garth chanted softly, absorbing essence from the ring. He felt the usual giddiness as power flooded his being, and he became invisible. Like something from a sci-fi movie, Garth simply faded into the background. Although he was invisible, he still had to be as quiet as possible. He still had his physical body, so he couldn't ignore the laws of physics and thrash about wildly without being heard, not without a sound-suppressing spell. Maybe the Citadel needed to create another ring that allowed the user to activate two different spells, he mused.

He was close to the archway at the entrance of the ranch when he heard footsteps approaching, and a voice saying calmly, "Identify yourself, and you won't be harmed."

Even though he knew the containment field was still active and O'Neal had assured him that the shield was intact, Mark was patrolling the perimeter of the ranch even.

He was dressed for combat in his black special forces outfit and his enchanted sword in a sheath strapped to his back. He had to agree with O'Neal's summation: the ranch was safe.

He was surprised at the doctor's contribution tonight. He had strengthened the door frames and windows of the house, making them virtually impossible to penetrate or destroy by anything less than a supernatural force. Considering their present trouble seemed to be of the straightforward, human variety, Mark was glad to have the bolt hole in case things went sideways.

Circling the ranch for the third time, Mark suddenly felt a presence approaching. He stretched out his essence and tensed up when he detected the use of magic. He hadn't expected to have to contend against any form of magic and having someone creep to the ranch in this way was disconcerting. He heard the door to the house open, and the rest of the group approached, including Isabella, who glared at Mark when their eyes met.

"You know you're safer in the house," he said, unable to ignore her blatant disregard for her own life. Isabella shrugged her shoulders, and Mark could tell from the defiant look on her face that arguing would be futile.

"What's going on? O'Neal warned us of someone coming." Gen stopped by Mark's side, and he saw the tip of the foot nail jutting from her fist. Mark stepped in front of the group, blocking the entrance to the ranch as he spoke.

"Identify yourself, and you won't be harmed."

Mark could sense that the figure had stopped some meters from the archway. A tense moment that seemed like hours passed. Just when he thought things were going to go south, a man appeared out of nothing. Even though Mark had sensed him and knew he was standing out there, he was still impressed with the magic. The gasps from the group behind him echoed his feelings.

Garth was shocked when the man he recognized from his research as Mark Reynolds ordered him to halt. For a moment, he thought the spell had failed, or the essence from his ring had been corrupted. But looking inward, Garth could see that everything was fine, and his invisibility spell was active.

Figuring he had been detected and trying to camouflage himself wasn't going to work anyway, Garth cancelled the spell and shimmered back into sight. Now he knew that the Citadel's information on Mark Reynolds was wrong. The report said that he was ex-special forces and owned a security outfit; nothing in it mentioned anything about him having magic, which Garth was a hundred percent sure he had used to spot him.

"I don't mean you any harm," he said. "My intentions are noble. You're harbouring a very dangerous individual, one of the four horsemen of the apocalypse. This man is the harbinger of death and destruction. I am only after him."

Garth was happy with his speech. He hadn't threatened anybody and had given them information they probably weren't aware of. No one in their right mind would want anything to do with Lucilius. There was no way they knew who he was and what he could do. Garth saw Mark cock his head as though thinking about what he had heard.

"I don't know who you're talking about, but I can guarantee you that there's no...member of the horsemen here. It would be better if you left the premises now."

Garth frowned in confusion. Did they not know what sort of creature resided in their midst? He needed to make these people understand the severity of the situation; Lucilius could plow through them like a harvester through a field of wheat. He opened his mouth to try again when one of the men in the group spoke out.

"He's talking about Lucilius."

The man that had spoken stood several steps behind the group, but Garth could feel Mark tense up, and the atmosphere around them became frigid. For a moment, he thought he saw the sword on Mark's back glow white, and a trail of white essence flowed into Mark's body. Garth blinked when a man standing to Mark's right stepped forward from the shadows.

Garth's eyes widened in disbelief and shock as he saw Lucilius standing in front of him. Everything clicked into place for him at that moment. Lucilius must have subverted these people, bent their wills somehow. It was unfortunate, but he would do what was necessary to take Lucilius down. If he had to take a few other lives in the process, it would still be a win.

In a single breath, Garth channelled his essence and covered himself in a shield. He pulled power from the remaining essence in the ring and winked out of human sight. Moments later, he shot a shield toward Lucilius.

Mark saw the man vanish but could still see his aura. He quickly pulled his sword from its sheath as he felt the man start to cast a spell. He glanced at Gen to make sure she was safe as he moved to engage the invisible man. The man cast his spell, and a shimmering blue cube raced through the air toward Lucilius. Mark didn't hesitate. He spun and struck the cube with his sword. There was a tinkling sound as it burst into tiny blue fragments.

"Lucilius, stay with Gen. Josephine, protect the group. O'Neal, back up Josephine as much as you can. I'll handle our invisible trespasser," Mark barked out his orders quickly and hoped the group would obey.

The invisible assailant turned his attention to Mark, shooting a short, glowing beam at him. Mark moved to the side, dodging the attack by inches. He didn't know what sort of magic the trespasser was using, but he didn't think getting hit by one of those beams would be fun. He sidestepped as he deflected the onslaught, advancing toward the trespasser.

Garth couldn't believe his eyes. He was shooting shield after shield at Mark, but somehow, the man kept avoiding them. He expected the soldier to dodge some of them but, considering the avalanche of beams; surely some should have hit him? He could feel the invisibility spell wearing off, so he enlarged his next shot. At the same time, he created a flat shield on the ground behind Mark.

When Mark stepped back to gauge how to respond to the shield coming at him, Garth smiled. He flicked his hand up, and the shield on the ground shot into the air, taking Mark with it. Garth turned his attention to the rest of the group, seeking out his target.

Mark sensed the beams of essence shooting toward him and weaved around them. Those he couldn't dodge, he destroyed with his sword. A larger one rushed at him, so he took a step back to prepare his strike, balancing the tip of his sword on the inside of his arm. Suddenly, Mark felt the ground propel him upward. He shot up into the air, reaching the height of the roof before he started plummeting back to the ground. He took a second to look down and saw the trespasser rush toward Gen and the rest of the group, most likely trying to get to Lucilius.

In a split second, Mark sorted through the memories of the protectors that came before him, looking for knowledge to help avoid breaking his legs when he fell. He came up blank but felt a thrumming from the sword in his hand. Was the weapon trying to tell him something? He didn't have time to ponder the question as the ground rose up to meet him. Drawing on pure instinct, he twisted in the air and pointed his sword downward. Just before impact, he poured essence into the weapon and blasted it at the ground, creating a shockwave that sent him flying a few feet up again. What would have been a deadly fall became a painful tumble as Mark landed and immediately rolled to his feet.

Gen watched Mark and, though she couldn't see the intruder anymore, knew they were battling ferociously. She glanced behind her at the rest of the team. Josephine had a determined look, and a grin on her face that worried Gen. O'Neal simply watched Mark move and parry.

"Can you see him?" Gen asked. She had a vague sense of where the intruder could be, but if O'Neal could see him, it would make things easier.

"He still remains invisible to my sight but based on Mark Reynolds's movements and my calculations of the possibilities, I can say that I can accurately pinpoint the intruder's position."

O'Neal spoke calmly, keeping his eyes glued on Mark. Gen didn't understand what he meant but was content to know that the group wasn't completely blind.

Suddenly, Mark shot into the air and flayed around wildly. She turned her head from side to side, trying to guess where the invisible man had gone. The nail in her palm grew warmer, and she lifted her clenched fist. No sooner had she done that than a force slammed into the shield around her.

Garth shot a beam at Gen and moved closer to his target. He could see Lucilius standing behind the group. That confirmed his suspicions that Mark, Gen, and the rest of the people on the ranch were thralls obeying Lucilius's will. He was amazed when his beam struck an invisible shield that had sprung up around Gen.

How could they have been this misinformed?
Could the horsemen gift others magic?

Even though his mind swarmed with questions, he didn't hesitate. He barreled into Gen and shoved her aside. He could see the confused looks on the faces of the group as he aimed a shield at Lucilius. It was thin and flat, and it shot toward Lucilius like a surgical needle.

O'Neal studied Mark's movements as he weaved around and swung his sword. The night lit up in brilliant blue sparks whenever Mark's sword struck something, and O'Neal used those moments to chart out potential outcomes. He went even further, mapping out possible coordinates to determine where the invisible man could be standing at any point in time. Slowly, an image started forming, and he could see the assailant's outline.

The man did something, and somehow Mark shot into the air. O'Neal wondered if he should be worried but decided it was more important to remain focused on the intruder. For a second, he lost sight of the invisible man's outline as a beam of essence slammed into the shield Gen had created.

That was an interesting development.

The nail in Gen's hand blazed with so much power that O'Neal had to look away to avoid being blinded by the glare. In that moment, the intruder was revealed, and O'Neal saw him shoot a thin beam of magic at Lucilius. He opened his mind to let the possibilities flood in and located the one that had Lucilius survive the encounter. He shoved Lucilius gently to the side, and the beam of energy shot ineffectually into the distance.

Suddenly, the intruder became fully visible as he stood in the center of the group, staring at Lucilius with hatred.

20

Myrddin used the distraction of the blaring alarm to gather his essence, then released a blast of air that swept out in a wide circle. The force threw the guards backward, some of them tumbling back into the bedroom from the balcony. When the force hit the blonde woman, she fell back, hitting the wall with a resounding thud. Amidst all the confusion, Marco stood quietly like a boulder in a shallow stream. The air hit him but billowed away into nothing. Myrddin saw the lining of his coat glow as the spell passed through him and understood that he must have laced his outfit with gold obsidian.

Marco snarled and rushed at him, moving faster than should have been possible for someone so large. Myrddin shot a dagger of air at him, which accomplished nothing, and ducked under the meaty arm that swung at his head.

A guard staggered to his feet and picked up his rifle, so Myrddin quickly created a shield around his body. The bullets hit moments later but didn't penetrate, and Myrddin sent out a spinning blade of air that sliced the rifle in two. He was glad he'd created the shield around his body as Marco punched him, but he staggered back under the force of the punch, and it shattered.

Myrddin swore as he saw Marco brandishing golden knuckledusters.

Just how many weapons did he have coated in the blasted obsidian? He leaned back to avoid another punch, thinking frantically, trying to decide on his next step. He couldn't attack Marco because of the gold obsidian he had on his person, and he couldn't take the giant in a one-on-one fight.

Another guard rushed onto the balcony, and Myrddin flicked his hand, sending half of the bisected rifle into his face. As the guard fell to the ground, it dawned on Myrddin that there was indeed a way to fight Marco.

Candice groaned in pain as her head hit the wall. The balcony grew fuzzy and dark as she struggled to maintain consciousness. She wondered how Merlin was still able to channel his magic despite the material Marco had told her about. She thought she'd advanced enough in her use of magic to be able to compete with her nemesis, but the blast of power that had hit her revealed how naïve she'd been.

The darkness lifted, and the world slowly came back into focus. Marco and Myrddin were still fighting. She stared in wonder as Marco stood steady, untouched by Myrddin's magic. It seemed that he had the ability to block all forms of magic. But, no, he wasn't blocking it she realized as she thought back to how Myrddin had flung the guards and herself aside. Somehow, Marco had rendered himself immune to it.

More guards poured onto the balcony, and Candice decided it was time to make a hasty exit. She stumbled down the stairs, her head still ringing from the collision with the wall. She reached the next floor down and hurried along the corridor. When she passed by the study, she thought she heard someone moving inside. Curious, she stopped. She had gotten the vibe that the study was Marco's sanctum sanctorum, and since the big man was fighting upstairs, it seemed someone else was poking around in there. Candice made her decision and returned to the study door. She turned the handle and pushed the door open slowly, immediately spotting the crumpled form of Marco's lanky assistant on the floor. His gun was lying next to his unconscious body. Picking it up, she heard a voice say, "I'm hoping you don't know how to use that, Miss."

Candice looked up and saw a short, sturdy man standing in front of the bookshelf. Then her eyes fell on the glass case clutched tightly under his arm.

Trosdan ran to the podium as the alarm blared. Deciding there wasn't any further need for finesse, especially as the room was filling with what he could only assume was toxic gas, he snatched the glass case from the podium.

The moment the glass lifted, he heard a grinding noise as the door started sliding shut. He grunted and ran back up the stairs as fast as he could. Myrddin hadn't said anything about running. Trosdan didn't like running. He got to the door just as it was about to slam shut and did the only thing a man in his position could do: he shoved his hand between the door and the doorframe.

He knew it was a stupid move, but he was desperate. The door pushed into his palm, and he bit his lip to stop himself from crying out. He thanked his mutation as his tough skin prevented the door from cutting into his hand, then braced his shoulder against the wall and began a tug-of-war with the door. The mechanism squealed in protest as the unstoppable force of the door met with an immovable object. After a minute's stalemate, it squeaked and slid back. Trosdan shoved his body into the gap and used the added leverage to push the door open. His muscles protested at the strain, but he pushed through the pain until the door opened completely. He slipped out and slammed the door shut behind him. Sagging back against the bookshelf, he took a well-deserved moment to catch his breath when the door to the study opened, and a blonde woman entered.

Trosdan watched quietly as she walked up to the unconscious man on the floor and picked up his gun.

"I'm hoping you don't know how to use that, Miss," he said as he struggled to his feet with the glass case underneath his arm. The woman straightened up and aimed the pistol at Trosdan. He didn't like the gleam in her eyes as she looked at the glass case.

"Put it down." The woman waved the gun at Marco's desk, but Trosdan hesitated. He'd gone through a lot to get the bloody case.

"I'm not going to say it again. Put the case over there."

Trosdan sighed but obeyed. He put the glass case on the desk.

"Look, Miss, why don't we—" Trosdan grunted in pain as he heard a loud bang. He stared at his chest in shock.

Had he been shot? Myrddin hadn't said anything about being shot.

The gun went off two more times, and Trosdan felt the force of the bullet fling him back against the bookshelf.

Candice grinned maniacally. She couldn't believe her good fortune. The moment she saw the glass case, she knew what it was. She didn't feel any remorse for killing the man. Nothing would stand in the way of her revenge. With the power of the crown of thorns,

Candice believed she'd finally surpass Merlin and be able to execute her plans to destroy him and all he held dear. He would know what it felt like to lose everything.

She walked to the desk and dropped the gun beside the case. Her hands shook slightly as she gazed at the relic she'd been searching for. As she reached out to grab the case, she felt pain shoot through her hand as something clasped her wrist.

"Now that wasn't friendly."

Candice couldn't believe her eyes. She hadn't missed. The bullets had hit the little man square in the chest. Yet here he was standing next to her— looking angry. The pain in her wrist intensified, and she screamed as her bones snapped under the pressure.

What kind of a monster stood before her?

Trosdan felt the bullets slam into his chest, and the bookshelf hit his back as he was thrown into it. Pain blossomed in his chest, but he could tell that the damage wasn't serious. His tough skin had acted as a bulletproof vest; it would take a much greater force to penetrate.

He saw the woman drop the gun on the desk and reach out for the glass case. Anger flared within him.

He remembered many years ago, as a teenager, when his mother had sat him down and told him about his heritage. His genetic mutation had become obvious, and he was a laughingstock among his peers. His skin began hardening in patches, and the discoloured blotches on his face and arms had made him look grotesque. He lashed out in anger at one of the boys that tormented him. The boy had been older and bigger, but when Trosdan hit him, he had doubled over and spat out blood. He later found out that the boy had broken four of his ribs and almost died.

He already knew about the skin mutation, but he wasn't aware that his family line also carried another inhuman trait. His mother explained that their anger brought uncommon strength and, if not tempered, could be very harmful. Trosdan had to learn how to control his temper and see the jovial side of life.

When Candice shot him, he wasn't angry, but when he saw her reaching for the glass case, rage exploded inside him. He didn't remember reaching out for her, and only her desperate scream of pain drove the rage from Trosdan's eyes.

"I'm so sorry, Miss," he apologized as Candice backed away from him, clutching her broken wrist gingerly.

Trosdan picked up the glass case and walked to the door as she cowered away from him.

"I am not a monster," Trosdan said softly as he walked out.

Myrddin prayed that their plan had succeeded as he channelled a lightning blast at the ground beside Marco. The floor erupted, cement flying in all directions. He created another shield to protect himself from the chunks of cement, but Marco staggered back under the rocky barrage.

The balcony looked like a warzone. Myrddin had used everything he could get his hands on to attack Marco, yet except for a little cut to his cheek and his dust-covered suit, the man still appeared unharmed. The suit had withstood everything he threw at it.

Myrddin heard a commotion from inside the room and grinned as Trosdan ran out onto the balcony.

"Whatever you're going to do, do it now!" Trosdan bellowed as he rushed at Myrddin.

Myrddin's essence was almost depleted, but he aimed another bolt of lightning at the wall behind Marco. The force of the blast created an explosion of brick, dust, and stone, forcing the giant to retreat from the debris that rained down. Myrddin grabbed Trosdan and headed for the edge of the balcony, preparing an invisibility spell.

Holding onto his friend's arm, Myrddin shot into the air. Trosdan had the fortitude to remain silent as the few remaining guards on the grounds opened fire. Myrddin extended his shield to cover them both as they headed for the closest wall. He knew he wouldn't be able to make it to the front gate, not at the rate he was burning through his essence. He gritted his teeth as his head started pounding. When they finally crossed the wall, Myrddin released the spell. They dropped to the ground, and Myrddin took a moment to catch his breath.

"Tell me you got it," Myrddin said between gulps of air. His head throbbed, and his chest felt constricted.

Trosdan showed Myrddin the glass case, and Myrddin gave his friend a thumbs-up. He hadn't really needed to ask the question, as he'd felt the power coming from the case.

"I know you're tired, but I don't think it's wise to hang around here," Trosdan said. "I don't know about you, but I don't think getting shot is any fun." Trosdan looked around as though expecting Marco's guards to jump out from the bushes.

Myrddin nodded, and together, they walked away from Marco Brambilla's villa.

21

CONSTANTINOPLE, 327 A.D.

No one stopped Remus as he walked through the palace gates.

The morning was bursting with people going about their day's work. He strolled through them with an air of authority, trying his best to mimic the person whose face he had stolen. Marius walked by his side, wearing a Praetorian guard uniform. He had no problem acting the part of someone who thought himself better than the men standing at the palace gates.

No one had an inkling of what they really looked like or who they were.

The plan was simple. Atticus and Lucilius would prepare a distraction to keep Merlin occupied. Meanwhile, Remus and Marius would infiltrate the palace and kill the nail bearer.

Simple, yet effective. As long as Calisto was out of the picture, the queen was as good as dead.

When they arrived at the queen's section of the palace, the guard stationed at the entrance stopped them.

"Password, Champion."

The guard had his hand on the pommel of his sword, but Remus could see that he wasn't expecting any trouble. This was all part of the usual routine. Nevertheless, Remus felt the first trickle of fear run down his spine since they had left the tavern earlier that night.

He didn't know the password.

"Champion?" The guard was more attentive now, and Remus knew if they were going to act, it had to be now. He prepared to bring out his bow from its enchanted hiding place. He was sure he could kill the guard before the guard could draw his sword, but if there were also guards on the other side of the archway, they'd be in trouble.

"Heron's wings bring swift flight," Marius said by his side. The guard relaxed and stepped aside for Remus and Marius to enter.

Remus breathed a sigh of relief as he walked into the courtyard beyond the entrance. He noticed that there were fewer servants in the queen's section of the palace than elsewhere but more guards. A lot more.

He wondered what had them so worked up. He understood that the four of them struck fear into the hearts of ordinary men, but this looked like overkill.

Surely the queen wasn't this afraid of the accursed?

A particularly alert-looking set of guards were stationed at a door off the courtyard, and he walked toward them. Marius fell into step by his side.

"Hail, Champion," one of the guards said. "The queen isn't in her chambers. The emperor sought her presence early this morning."

Remus nodded.

They would wait for the queen's return. Today, she would meet her maker.

Merlin was walking down a narrow path in the center of the city, trying to avoid getting jostled by the crowds of people around him. If it had been a market day, it would have been impossible to advance more than a few steps every ten minutes. Luckily, today was just an ordinary day in Constantinople. To everyone else, anyway.

He would have answers soon. An informant from Calisto's network of spies had sent word that another cell had been found, and Merlin hoped to use this information to track down the person behind the cult movement. He didn't believe Derog was the one responsible for the rash of killings or the beasts and entities that had been summoned.

Derog was a magical cripple with a shattered essence; the worst punishment that could be meted out to any person that used magic. Merlin had never seen anyone recover from that. No, someone else had to be pulling the strings.

He had also dismissed the idea that the accursed could be behind the ritual practices. It wasn't as though the accursed didn't have the know-how, but as he'd told Queen Helena, the accursed believed in self-gratification. They wanted to kill the queen themselves.

Merlin reached the end of the path and came to a crossroads. The informant had said to look out for a house with red markings on the windowsill. He glanced both ways and spotted a windowsill with red stripes. He turned to his right, about to head in that direction, when he stopped.

He felt an inexplicable urge to go the other way instead.

He sensed danger. Someone important to him was in danger, and that could only mean the queen. He spun around to retrace his steps back to the palace, but then he stopped again. The urge to go left at the crossroad was too strong. Merlin gave in to the compulsion and raced down the street, his robes billowing behind him. Startled townsfolks hurriedly leapt aside to get out of his way. The urge was strong, and though he couldn't tell what it meant, he had learned to trust that feeling over the years. The same intuition had saved him numerous times and had even shown him glimpses of the future.

He stopped in front of a tavern. The sense of danger was very strong here, and he stretched out his senses to feel traces of familiar, dark tendrils.

The accursed had been here.

Merlin shielded himself and prepared a wind

spell in his hands. He stretched out his right hand and blew the door open. After waiting a few seconds for a counter-spell that didn't appear, Merlin walked in.

The inside of the tavern was in shadows, as the shutters were closed, but Merlin could make out a human form in a corner of the room. It released a familiar essence.

"Calisto?" Merlin whispered.

He waited for a response, but the form remained silent and impassive. He walked over slowly, checking his personal shield to make sure it was intact. He released another wind spell to turn the form around and blow away the shroud of darkness that covered it.

It was Calisto, gagged and tied. Merlin quickly untied his restraints and helped the protector to his feet.

"The queen is in danger," Calisto blurted out.

"What happened?"

"The accursed. They sprang a trap. They plan to assassinate the queen. Remus took my form. He went with Marius. I heard them say they were preparing a distraction for you. We need to hurry."

Merlin nodded grimly, grateful he had listened to his gut. There would have been no hope of stopping the accursed if he'd ignored his premonition. He would have been held up fighting Atticus and Lucilius while Remus and Marius carried out their plan to assassinate the queen.

The two men hurried out of the tavern and started running.

Remus was getting tired of waiting.

He was leaning against a wall, repeatedly flipping his dagger into the air and catching it. This game earned him some wary glances from the guards, but he didn't care.

He was bored and needed to do something. Anything to reduce the monotony of standing in one place and staring at the same face for hours.

Standing guard wasn't for him, and obviously, it was beneath Calisto too. One of the guards suggested that the champion had more pressing matters to attend to.

What could be more pressing than protecting the frustrating nail bearer?

Remus spun a dagger in the air once more and caught it by the handle.

Calisto panted heavily as he reached the palace gate. Merlin stopped beside him, less winded than he was.

The wizard must be using magic somehow, he thought, wishing he had a trick like that up his sleeve. He took deep gulps of air to steady his beating heart and get his emotions in check.

One of the guards fumbled a quick salute, but the other frowned.

"Champion? Did you leave through the south gate?"

Calisto appreciated the guard's attention to detail and made a mental note to remember him. The queen needed such observant men around her.

Calisto simply nodded, as he didn't want to waste time explaining who he was and who had passed through the gates earlier. Merlin had explained to Calisto that it was important to keep the existence of the accursed secret.

The guards stepped aside to let them pass, and they walked briskly toward the queen's section of the palace.

"What's the plan?" Calisto asked.

"Get in there, blast the accursed to little smidgeons, or something in that vein."

"In other words, we don't have a plan."

"That would also be accurate. Do you have anything?"

Calisto shook his head. "There have been more guards around the queen's chambers since the demon's attack. Some may be susceptible to Marius's persuasion. We may have to fight more than the two accursed. Can we get them with your sleep spell?"

"It will be taxing," Merlin said. "But remember, Remus and Marius are resilient when it comes to magic. The spell might not affect them."

"But then we'll only have the two of them to deal with."

"It will be two-on-one for a while, as I'll need some minutes to recover."

Calisto considered Merlin's words. He would have been more worried if Lucilius or Atticus were present. Marius's powers were useless against him, so that left only Remus.

"I think I can handle myself against those two," Calisto said.

"Then we have a plan."

Remus was starting to go stir-crazy. He was just considering killing someone to alleviate his boredom when he heard footsteps approaching. The guards stood to attention as Queen Helena and two other guards entered the courtyard.

He breathed a sigh of relief as he watched the queen approach her bed chamber. He and Marius would have to keep their distance, as the queen would sense their presence if they got too close.

That would spoil everything and ruin their plans.

Queen Helena stopped by the door, and Remus saw her frown. She looked around at the courtyard, and Remus and Marius turned their faces away.

"Calisto?"

The queen took a step toward Remus, then stopped. He watched with bated breath as she turned around and walked to her bed chamber.

Queen Helena couldn't stop shaking as she shut the door behind her.

She had sensed the darkness surrounding the imposter that had taken Calisto's place. It had to be the shapeshifter, Remus. The accursed were here to kill her, and she was alone. Calisto and Merlin hadn't returned since they left to put a stop to the growing presence of the cult movement in the city.

Helena brought out the nail she kept close to her body at all times.

She drew comfort from the warm sensation of the nail in her palm. Whispering a silent prayer, she clutched it tightly and backed away from the door.

Remus didn't know how he knew, but he suspected that the nail bearer was on to them.

"I think she knows," he whispered to Marius.

"It doesn't matter. Her protectors are nowhere to be seen. She dies tonight."

Remus agreed silently, and they walked to the queen's door.

"Password?"

Calisto and Merlin had reached the archway leading to the queen's personal chambers.

The guard looked up and saw Calisto's face.

"Imposter!" he shouted, bringing his spear to bear, but Calisto was too close. He gripped the man's face and slammed his head against the archway. The second guard managed to point his sword in Calisto's direction, but Merlin summoned a strong wind to toss the guard aside.

Calisto entered the courtyard and saw Remus and Marius nearby the queen's bed chamber.

"Kill the imposters!" Remus yelled.

"Don't let them get near the queen!" Marius commanded. "We will protect her from inside."

Remus and Marius entered the queen's bed chamber as the guards surrounded Calisto and Merlin.

"Now would be an excellent time for the sleep spell, Wizard." Calisto deflected a punch and gripped the attacking guard's arm, swinging him against another.

Merlin thrummed with power.

"SLEEP!" he bellowed.

The guards dropped like puppets who had their strings cut. Calisto jumped over the bodies as he rushed for the queen's bed chamber.

He prayed he wasn't too late.

Remus and Marius rushed into the room to see the nail bearer waiting for them, pointing the foot nail at them.

"I will take you with me today." Queen Helena tried to still the trembling in her hands and the quiver in her voice. It wouldn't do for the accursed to know just how afraid she was. She felt like she might faint, but she was determined not to give in to her fear or have the two men before her take pleasure in her despair.

"Where is your protector, oh great queen?" Marius taunted. "I told you I'd get my revenge, didn't I? You will beg me to kill you before the day is over."

Helena glared at Marius with disgust. She could hear the joy in his voice at her predicament. She firmed her resolve and aimed the nail at the two immortals, ready to give them the fight of their lives.

"Let's do what we came to do, Marius. The wizard and the protector are coming," Remus said nervously.

Helena took courage from his words. If she could stall them, maybe she could still make it through the next few minutes.

"You may kill me, but I can guarantee you, you are also dying today," Queen Helena spat. "This chamber is warded against your kind." She watched Remus frown with doubt and turned to address him directly. "There is nowhere to run. Be assured that your end comes today."

Helena heard rushing footsteps outside and hoped it was her protector and the wizard, or anyone that could aid her against the accursed.

"Do it now," Remus snarled, pulling out his bow.

Helena stared wide-eyed as he nocked an arrow.

Then the door burst open.

The force of the kick almost removed the door from its hinges. Calisto somersaulted into the bed chamber and felt the air displace above him as an arrow flew over his head. He got to his feet, rage twisting his face into a snarl. He saw Remus take another shot, but he shifted his stance, and the arrow missed him. Three more arrows flew at him but encountered only air.

Calisto danced around in a blur of movement, deflecting another arrow with his sword. He was getting close to Remus, but he kept one eye on Marius. He saw the accursed rush at Queen Helena.

Marius was seething with rage.

Why wouldn't they allow him to get his revenge? His words of power were useless against the nail bearer and her protector.

He could feel the protector's fury like a hot blast from a furnace.

Queen Helena glanced at the fight behind him, and he used the opportunity to strike. One cardinal rule of battle always rang true: never take your eyes off your opponent.

Marius pulled out the sword sheathed by his side, preparing to plunge it into Queen Helena's stomach to deliver what would surely be a death blow. His aim was true and his hand firm, yet somehow, he missed, and he merely grazed the nail bearer's gown.

He looked down and saw a sword embedded in

his side. Shock registered on his face as he realized that he had disobeyed the other cardinal rules himself. He had taken his eyes off his opponent. Marius looked up and met Calisto's triumphant gaze.

He fell to one knee. He could still do this, he told himself. He looked up to see the queen clutching her dress to her side, where a red stain was spreading.

Had he succeeded after all?

Queen Helena staggered toward him.

"Today, we rid the world of your kind," she said in a cold voice.

Marius stared up at Helena, his eyes widening as she plunged the nail into his chest.

He screamed, falling back on the floor as pain washed over him.

Helena watched Marius flailing around on the floor as he tried to remove the nail, but it burrowed into his chest until it couldn't be seen anymore.

A final convulsion shook his body, and he grew still. His corpse instantly began to wither and dry as he aged swiftly. Within seconds, only a pile of ashes remained where Marius's body had been.

Calisto saw Marius going in for the kill and did the only thing that came to his mind.

Protect the queen at all costs.

He didn't hesitate. He flung his sword at Marius. It spun in the air before striking home, piercing the accursed's side. Content that he'd taken the immortal out of the picture, for the time being, Calisto turned back to face the other accursed.

Remus hadn't been idle; he released an arrow aimed right at Calisto's heart.

Calisto saw his death flying toward him and shifted his stance again, twisting to the side to present a smaller target. The arrow trailed a path of pain across his chest and struck the wall with a thud.

Ignoring the ache, he turned back to Remus, but the immortal chose that moment to reveal his true colours. He ran through the door, bumping into Merlin as he fled.

Calisto thought of chasing after the immortal but decided to tend to Queen Helena instead, who had taken a seat on her bed.

He walked over and joined her, nodding, and she returned a weary smile.

Merlin entered the bedroom and placed his hands on Calisto's shoulder.

"Attend to the queen first. I think she may be hurt," he told the wizard. He had seen Marius strike at Helena and wasn't sure if she was hurt. But Merlin kept his hand on Calisto's shoulder until the wound knitted up.

When Merlin turned his attention to the queen, Calisto walked over to Marius's ashes and rummaged through the pile with his fingers. He found the nail and brushed off the traces of ash that clung to it, then walked back to the bed and handed it to Helena.

"I never thought I'd get to see this day." Merlin leaned against one of the wooden bed posts.

"The death of an immortal?" Calisto asked.

"Yes. You did well, Queen Helena."

"It wasn't me. It was the power of the foot nail."

"A power that could only be activated by you, my queen. History will sing your praises for ridding the world of Marius."

Helena nodded.

She closed her fist around the nail, taking comfort in the fact that it had achieved the impossible. She also knew the time had come for her to do what had been weighing so heavily on her soul.

"My time is close, Wizard."

"What do you mean?" Merlin had an inkling of what the queen was hinting at, but he hadn't thought it would happen for many years to come.

"The burden needs to be passed on to someone else, Merlin. I can feel my time nearing its end."

"No. You will live long, my queen," Calisto protested.

"I'm not saying I'm dying, Calisto, but I've been wondering…what will happen after I'm gone? A new nail bearer will have to be found, and she'll be all alone in this. She'll have no one to help her understand what is happening to her. If we can find the next nail bearer now, she will benefit from my wisdom and experience."

"You aren't dying yet, Queen Helena," Merlin said. "We can talk about this at a later date."

"You need to know who the next nail bearer will be, Wizard," the queen insisted. "What if the accursed somehow find out who it is? The task still falls on the two of you to protect her."

Merlin nodded. Helena turned to Calisto, but her protector had walked to the door.

"Will the guards wake up soon?" he asked.

"Give me a minute or two to rest. We'll wake them up then. I don't think we need to expect any trouble from the accursed for a while."

Helena nodded, but she felt uneasy. The death of one of the accursed would definitely sow confusion amongst them, but another emotion would also be ignited: rage.

22

Mark sprang to his feet when he sensed the presence of multiple bodies rapidly approaching the ranch. The strike team had arrived.

He ran back to Gen and the rest of the group. The intruder was now visible and was clearly about to release a massive spell.

"We have incoming!" he yelled as he reached the group.

The spell released, and he swung his sword, shattering the large shield the intruder had created. He stared at Mark with a dazed expression.

"We don't have time for this." Mark slammed the pommel of his sword across the intruder's head, and the man slumped to the ground.

He needed to make a decision, and he needed to do it quickly. The strike team was nearing the group's position by the archway.

"We need to retreat," Mark whispered.

"Why?" Lucilius snapped. "We still have the element of surprise."

"But not the terrain to benefit from it." Mark had hoped to form a pincer group that would trap the attacking teams in the middle, but it was too late now. Their timing was off.

"We retreat to the house and use that to our advantage. We know the layout better than they do." Mark could see that Lucilius wanted to argue, but Gen spoke up. "We listen to Mark. Let's go." She headed for the house, and the rest of the group followed. Mark bent down and lifted the intruder onto his shoulders. The man would have a lot to answer for later.

Patrick scanned the area with his night-vision goggles. He lifted his fist, and his team halted behind him. The ranch looked deserted, but the infrared imagery showed that the inhabitants had taken shelter in the house.

He raised two fingers, letting his team know that they were to split into two groups, then gestured toward the front door for the first team and the back of the house for the second.

With the first team following him, Patrick headed to the front door.

Mark spread his essence wide and sensed the strike force dividing into two groups.

"One half of their team is heading for the back; the other is coming at us from the front. We need to split up," he told the group. The challenge would be how to split their group to make the best of their different abilities.

"I'll take the team heading for the back. The rest of you handle the front." He saw Gen shaking her head, but he stopped her. "You know I can handle myself, and I need you to take care of the others. Your shield will come in handy too."

Gen was silent for a second. Then she quietly said, "Be careful."

"You too." He turned and glanced at Lucilius, who returned his look. Mark nodded, content that Gen would have someone watching her back.

"Try not to stress yourself out," he told Josephine, but the young woman simply snorted and shook her head.

Mark sighed and headed for the back door. He needed to lure the team away from the house.

Gen watched Mark go and almost chased after him. They'd never separated during a battle before, and she didn't think doing so now was the right move. And leaving her in charge of the group?

"He is going to be okay, Nail Bearer. We should worry about ourselves," she heard Lucilius say. The others nodded in agreement, and she had to concur. Mark could take care of himself.

She looked at the faces around her again. She, Josephine, and O'Neal were the only ones with abilities, and among the three of them, none had an offensive power. Mark always took on that role, which meant for them to survive, they would have to adapt.

"I don't know how strong the front door is, even with O'Neal's reinforcements, or what these people will use to try and break it down, so we have to be prepared. Isabella, you may have to sit this one out." Gen was happy that Isabella didn't argue; she nodded and headed for the living room.

"I'll be our shield while Lucilius attacks from a distance. Josephine, since you can only use your ability a few times, hold back and make sure things don't go badly for us."

Josephine nodded, and Gen turned to O'Neal.

"O'Neal, you just continue to be you."

Lucilius didn't agree with Mark's plan, and he definitely didn't think he should have left the nail bearer unguarded. Leaving the nail bearer with him was the same as leaving her without any protection at all. He was a shadow of his former self and didn't think anyone should be placed in his care.

Looking to his left, he saw O'Neal standing perfectly still with a characteristically inscrutable expression on his face. Lucilius didn't understand the full scope of what the man could do but felt sure that the former doctor's abilities weren't yet fully utilized. And he hadn't missed the fact that O'Neal had saved his life earlier when the intruder targeted him.

Lucilius was preoccupied—filled with bitterness at envy while Mark defended the group—when he had felt O'Neal shove him aside. Moments later, the intruder became visible, and judging by the man's position and the hatred in his eyes, Lucilius knew he would have been killed if the doctor hadn't intercepted.

So, O'Neal should have been the one tasked with keeping the nail bearer safe, not him.

His thoughts were interrupted when he heard a loud boom that shook the front door.

Mark opened the back door and snuck outside just as the strike team made it around the side of the house. He pulled out his sword and activated his abilities, sifting through memories and skills. He settled on one of the memories of his ancestor, Protector Shu Hang. One of the previous nail bearers was from the Far East, and her protector was a renowned warrior who specialized in close combat.

Memories flooded Mark's mind and seeped into his muscles. As he rushed at the assailants, they raised their weapons to open fire. The squad members were packing high-powered assault weapons that would be lethal if brought to bear. The only problem was that they were bulky and impractical in confined spaces or up close to your target, involving a significant risk of unwanted collateral damage.

Mark slashed his sword, cutting through the first weapon. He lashed out with his right foot and landed a kick on the now weaponless assailant's abdomen. The force slammed the man into another attacker behind him, and both went sprawling.

This time drawing from the sword's power, Mark activated another skill, and his senses sharpened to a superhuman level. He was aware of the leaves on distant trees as they swayed in the night breeze. He could hear the thudding heartbeats of the men gathered to kill him. The sound of a bullet entering the chamber was deafening.

The attackers seemed to be moving sluggishly, and Mark realized that his heightened senses also sped up his movement and perception. He knew the ability wouldn't last, but he didn't need long to put it to good use.

The air around him was displaced as a bullet spun toward him. He bent at the waist and moved his shoulders slightly, and the shell whisked past him. He thrust out his sword, destroying another weapon.

Mark moved around the six men in a blur, the clattering sound of shattered weapons falling to the ground filling the night air.

The men looked at their empty hands, baffled
and afraid, as Mark sheathed his sword. His senses
and speed were returning to normal as his ability
waned. He wasn't concerned. The rest of the fight,
he could do on his own.

Another boom shook the door, and Gen was certain that the next one would rip it off its hinges. She
braced herself against it, pouring all her will and
determination into activating her shield. The door
slammed into her defence with another boom, and
Gen grunted with the effort of maintaining it. She
remembered her vision and bent her knees to absorb
the impact of the next collision.

The force proved too much for the door, and it
shattered into pieces. But Gen's shield held.

She used the brief moment of respite following
the explosion to check on the group. She nodded
confidently at the determined faces staring at her
and turned back to the gaping doorway. Gen was
now the shield protecting her family, and no enemy
would get past her. She took a few steps back, her
shield moving with her. Red beams crisscrossed the
hallway, and she braced herself for the inevitable
barrage of gunfire.

Josephine didn't know what she could do to affect the flow or outcome of the fight. She could reverse time, but that didn't seem to be needed presently. Gen stood in front of them, a bulwark against the flood of enemies. Bullets ping-ponged around the narrow hallway, and she heard one of the attackers scream in pain. A voice called a ceasefire, and silence filled the house.

One of the men stepped forward and reached out to touch Gen's shield. He gently placed a hand on the translucent wall that blocked them from the group, and Josephine heard him whisper something in amazement.

"I don't know who you are or how you can do this, but will you survive if we blow up the house?" The man gave a hand signal to his team behind him, and a small robotic vehicle zoomed into the hallway with a mechanical whine.

"This is a modified **MAARS** robot. It was designed for bomb disposal, but this one has been modified for bomb dispersal. Drop this…barrier, and I can guarantee that no one else will be hurt."

"What about Gen?" Josephine shouted.

"Sorry, Miss, but a job's a job. We're only here for Genesis Isherwood. Nobody else has to get hurt."

Josephine saw the look of indecision on Gen's face and shook her head.

"You can't think they'll keep to their word Gen. And even if they will, you don't get to sacrifice yourself for us."

"What if it's the only way I can be sure that the rest of you are safe?"

"That's utter rubbish, Gen; stick to the plan. Think what Mark would say." Josephine was glad to see her words seemed to have made an impact as Gen addressed the man standing on the other side of the shield.

"No," she said flatly. "My counteroffer is that you leave. Before things get very bad for you."

The man tapped his foot as he tried to stare Gen down. "You leave me with no choice then." He turned to the man behind him. "Bring in Mark Reynolds. We'll execute him here."

Josephine stared in disbelief as they manhandled Mark into the hallway, a hood over his head. They shoved him to his knees. Josephine shouted a warning as Gen moved toward him.

She stared in horror as the kneeling man brought out a gun and aimed it at Gen's chest.

That's not Mark.

A shot rang out, and Gen staggered backward and hit the wall. Josephine screamed silently, stretched out her hand, and twisted it in the air.

Gen jerked upright and moved back to where she had been standing. The kneeling man got to his feet and was dragged out of the room. Josephine felt the strain of using her ability to defy the natural progression of time, and she let go when the man started walking toward Gen's shield.

The conversation played out again, and when the man started tapping his foot, Josephine took her chance.

"Whatever he says next shouldn't be believed," she said. "Gen, please don't drop your shield. They'll bring in an imposter to try and get to you, but Mark is fine."

Josephine saw a look of confusion and shock cross the man's face. Then he snarled and raised his rifle. He emptied the clip at Gen's shield, which didn't so much as crack.

"You cannot keep this up," the man yelled.

"They won't have to," Mark said from behind the men, and Josephine felt like whooping in victory.

Mark drove a cupped palm into the nose of the last attacker standing, and the man slumped to the ground. He looked at the men lying around him, some unconscious, others groaning in pain. Having held back his punches and tried not to injure the attackers too badly, Mark finished off the fight as quickly as possible when he heard gunshots coming from the house.

The gunfire ceased abruptly, and he felt his heartbeat spike. He ran for the house, breathing a sigh of relief when he heard muffled voices and recognized one of them as Gen's.

When he reached the porch, he dropped to one knee to survey the situation. The other half of the task team had breached the front door and infiltrated the hallway. A few men were gathered by the door, watching what was unfolding inside.

Mark crept up behind the man at the back of the group and silently grabbed him, covering his mouth and lifting him off his feet as he dragged him away. He shifted his grip to a neck lock and applied pressure. The man struggled briefly before passing out. Mark crouched by the fallen man, listening to hear if he'd been discovered.

The comforting sound of talking continued inside the house as Mark did the impossible. One by one, he ambushed the remaining members of the strike team and knocked them unconscious. Finally, only the man talking to Gen was left, oblivious to what had been going on behind his back.

Another round of gunshots rang out, but Mark wasn't too worried. Closer, now, he could hear the conversation. The man had grown frustrated and was shooting futilely at the shield Gen had created.

"You cannot keep this up."

Mark heard the defeat in his voice and knew the man was broken. He wouldn't make another attempt at the ranch.

"They won't have to."

The man spun around. It was the leader of the strike team, and he now had his rifle aimed at Mark. The click of an empty chamber filled the corridor, and his eyes widened. He looked around and realized that all his men were either dead or incapacitated.

"They aren't dead. But we both know that you won't be lucky a third time. You're done. The police are on the way."

Finally dropping her shield, Gen rushed to Mark, and he opened his arms to receive her hug. He watched over her shoulder as Lucilius walked up to the strike team's leader and knocked him unconscious with the butt of the gun in his hand.

They had survived another attack.

23

C andice cradled her broken wrist as she walked into the hidden room underneath Marco Brambilla's study. She looked around the bare space, wondering what she was hoping to find.

The crown of thorns was gone, taken from her grasp. Her wrist throbbed with pain. She gritted her teeth and swallowed. She had known fear in her life, but looking at the man who had crushed her bones, brought on a level of despair she hadn't thought possible. His eyes had gleamed red, and in the smoke and confusion, he looked like a demon about to rip her soul from her body.

The alarm blaring interrupted her thoughts, and she shook her head, willing herself to focus.

The room had nothing to offer. She was about to head back up the stairs when she saw a small wooden box in the corner of the room. The box was barely larger than an average vanity case and seemed out of place in the otherwise empty room. Candice dragged herself to the box and knelt beside it.

Like everything else in the villa, the box was unlocked. Marco believed a show of strength was enough to deter even the most determined from robbing him. That pride seemed to be the giant's only weakness, and as Candice opened the box, she was grateful for that flaw. The box shone with a golden brilliance, and Candice felt the strength drain from her body.

Whatever was in the box was absorbing her life essence, making her feel as helpless as she'd felt when she'd first come into the villa.

"What are you doing here?" Marco barked in Italian.

Candice shut the wooden box and struggled to her feet.

"It seems you've been keeping secrets from me. And here I thought we were partners." Candice tried to sound flippant but retreated as Marco walked deeper into the room.

"We are not partners. We are not equals. I command; you follow." The words were stated flatly and without emotion, and Candice felt herself nodding in agreement. Marco radiated rage, and she didn't want it directed at her. She noted that his suit was covered in dust and plaster; some of it even clung to his face.

"The wizard dies tonight. My men have annexed the city, and we will find him." Marco glared at Candice as though hoping she'd contradict him, but she kept quiet as she watched the leader of the Brambilla dynasty storm up the stairs and out of the hidden room. She followed quietly behind. She felt a sliver of fear as she realized that finding the wizard would also mean the wizard finding them.

Myrddin flopped down on the hotel bed and covered his eyes with his arm. The journey back from the villa had been uneventful, but he knew he needed to get out of town before Marco found him. He had already packed his small duffel bag and was ready to go to the airport when he heard his phone ring, and he groaned as he took it from his pocket.

When Myrddin saw the caller's name, a smile lit his weary face. He answered the call.

"Hello, Sunshine. I'm on my way."

During their brief conversation, he assured Gen that his trip had been successful and that he would be home soon.

The call ended, and Myrddin dropped the phone on the mattress beside him. His headache wasn't going away. Shielding Trosdan had been difficult, as the spell kept washing over him and fizzling into nothing, so

Myrddin compensated by shielding the air around Trosdan instead and constantly adjusting it as they moved. The improvised adjustment had been taxing, both physically and mentally, and drained him quickly and dramatically.

He knew rest would rectify the essence overburn, so he decided to sleep for just a little while before it was time to go to the airport.

Myrddin woke up with a start.

He didn't know how long he'd been asleep, but his head was still pounding, and his essence was still below half-full. He opened his eyes and groggily took in his surroundings.

What had woken him up? Myrddin cast his essence outside of his hotel room. At first, everything seemed normal, but the absolute silence suggested otherwise. He stretched his senses further and heard the ding of the elevator as the door slid open, followed by the soft thudding of soled shoes on thick carpet.

Myrddin sprang to his feet and groaned as the room swam before his eyes. He leaned against the wall to steady himself as he counted the men running for his hotel room. He stopped counting when he reached eight.

It seemed Marco's reach went even further than he had realized.

The men didn't hesitate. They kicked down the door, hoping to subdue Myrddin with their greater numbers.

The wizard chanted as the door flew open, and the first two men through the door screamed in agony as blinding light flooded the room. Myrddin heard the ominous clicks as the rest of the men cocked their guns and aimed them at him. Quickly, he cast a shield of solid air around his body, and gunshots filled the bedroom.

Ordinarily, Myrddin wouldn't have been bothered by the men's feeble attempts to bring him down, but he was still recovering from his encounter with Marco at the villa. He struggled to maintain the shield around him, waiting desperately for the men to run out of ammunition.

The final click of an empty chamber rang through the air. Myrddin wove his hands in an intricate pattern as he cast another spell, imbuing it with as much essence as he could spare.

Blue lightning raced out of his fingers and struck the attackers. The light jumped from body to body in an arc that left its victims in spasms as they hit the floor. Myrddin breathed rapidly, taking large gulps of air to steady himself.

There was only one sure way an ordinary, mundane human could overwhelm a magic user: bombard the magician with bodies. Eventually, the magic user would suffer essence overburn and succumb to the human.

It seemed Marco Brambilla was aware of that strategy. Myrddin sensed another team of human fighters pouring into the hotel, and he was sure they would not be the last.

Hoping Trosdan was okay, he prepared for the next bout.

Trosdan shoved a few items of clothing into a duffel bag and zipped it up hurriedly.

It was time to get out of dodge.

He wouldn't have tangled with Marco for anyone, no matter the reward or the cause. But Myrddin wasn't just anyone.

Trosdan had lived a long life, and over the years, he had realized that good friends were few and far between. Merlin, or Myrddin, as he liked to be called now, had been there for him numerous times before, but Trosdan could count the number of times he'd come to the wizard's aid on one hand. In other words, he owed Myrddin. And he was happy to pay back his debt. Getting the crown of thorns away from a man like Marco Brambilla was an added bonus.

He looked around the small bedroom and, not seeing anything else of value, he rushed through the narrow corridor and pulled open the front door.

It took a moment to register the men standing outside the door, but only another microsecond to react to the punch aimed at his face.

It was an awkward blow, as Trosdan was a couple of feet shorter than the man who struck at him. He angled his face to the side, and the edge of the man's fist grazed his cheek. The punch missed.

Trosdan threw his duffel bag at the intruder and tried to slam the door shut. The attackers yelled and rushed forward, pushing with their combined weight before it could close. Trosdan yelled and pressed back against the door with his shoulder, feeling it slide slowly toward the wooden frame. With a final burst of energy, he slammed it shut and turned the lock. He heard a satisfying click as the door lock activated. He turned around to see the butt of a gun bearing down on him, and the world went dark.

24

arth woke up in stages.

Once he gained consciousness, he remained still and made sure his breathing didn't change. He needed a moment to assess the situation. He was upright and could feel the pressure of a wooden chair against his back. Some type of rope was wound around his chest, securing him to the seat.

He had failed to kill one of the horsemen of the apocalypse. Why was he still alive?

Not only alive but feeling better than he had in a long time.

"You can open your eyes now. We know you're awake." The voice was quiet and calm, and Garth felt himself obeying without question.

He blinked and saw six pairs of eyes staring at him. He ignored their glares and looked around to take in his surroundings.

He was in what appeared to be a repurposed barn. A few feet in front of him stood the man who could see through his invisibility spell, observing him quietly.

Beside him was a pretty young woman with flaming red hair. Four other people stood to either side of the couple, one he immediately recognized as Lucilius.

"You do not know who you have in your midst." Garth struggled against his restraints, but he couldn't loosen the rope. The man in front of him quickly glanced at Lucilius before turning his attention back.

"Why did you attack us?" he asked.

"He is an abomination. I am only after him, but it's obvious he has a hold over the rest of you. Lucilius needs to die."

"No one needs to die," the woman with the red hair said. "Release him."

The man next to her frowned and then sighed. He walked over to Garth and leaned down to untie the knots that held the ropes in place.

"It won't end well for you if I see you gather a drop of essence."

The words were spoken softly, but Garth felt his heart speed up as fear blossomed within him. He didn't doubt the truth of the man's words. He knew the man would be able to sense any attempt he made to use magic.

The question was if he was willing to sacrifice his life for another chance to end Lucilius.

"Hi, my name is Gen. This tall, brooding gentleman is Mark. Behind us are Josephine, Isabella, and O'Neal. Lucilius, you already know."

Garth stared in amazement as the woman with red hair introduced the group. They each waved casually when their names were mentioned, except Lucilius, who seemed bored with the show of camaraderie.

Garth loosened the untied rope around his chest and started to get to his feet, but the man, Mark, pushed him back down.

"Not yet. You know who we are, so why don't you start by introducing yourself?"

He looked into Mark's resolute eyes and knew it was best to play along for now. "The name's Garth, Garth Armstrong," he said.

"Okay, Garth. I can only assume why you attacked us, but that reason is wrong. Lucilius isn't who he once was," Gen said.

"That is impossible," he snorted. "He is an accursed. One of the four horsemen of the apocalypse. The agents of destruction and one of the dark one's knights. He deserves death," Garth stated flatly.

"You are right," Lucilius spoke up for the first time. Garth tried to stand again, but Mark held him down, so he could only watch warily as Lucilius walked up to him.

Would this be the moment he was turned into a mindless thrall like the others? As though reading his thoughts, Lucilius stopped beside Gen and shoved his hands into his pockets.

"You are right. I deserve death. I have done things that I deserve to die a thousand deaths for. You think they are under my spell? It's the other way around. I don't know why I was given a second chance, but I was. I can't change my past, but I'm hoping I'll be able to make something of my future, no matter how fleeting that may be."

Lucilius nodded at Mark, who took a couple of steps back, and Garth slowly rose to his feet. It seemed he was being tested, and he wasn't sure that was a wise call. He took a chance and created a shield around his body. Garth noticed Mark assume a defensive stance, but he remained still.

Garth felt the tension in the barn increase as he weighed his options.

He could strike Lucilius down right now if he wanted to. Were they telling the truth? Was he a changed man? Was it even possible for an accursed to change?

He sighed inwardly. That was the problem. No, he didn't believe an accursed could be redeemed.

In a swift move that would have pleased his instructor, Garth shaped a needle-like shield and shot it at Lucilius's heart.

Better safe than sorry.

Mark hadn't been comfortable releasing Garth, but he'd learned to trust Gen's instinct and was ready for any sudden or threatening move from their prisoner. He listened carefully as Lucilius poured out his feelings.

He understood wanting redemption for past crimes. The confession gave Mark more respect for the former immortal and erased any lingering doubts about his motives.

Mark had spread out his essence in the barn before Garth had woken up. Although the attack had been sudden and the others didn't expect it, he had been ready for such a gambit.

But as Mark saw essence pour out of Garth, he wished he'd ignored Gen's suggestion to leave his sword behind. She thought that waving a sword in their captive's face would undermine their peaceful greeting.

Mark was fast, but as he ran toward Lucilius, he realized he'd underestimated Garth's speed. He felt anger rise within him as he saw the look of acceptance on Lucilius's face. The former immortal figured Garth wouldn't believe his story, and he was ready to accept judgment.

Mark slammed into Lucilius, and the sharp bolt of magic hit both of them. A sharp pain spread through his side, and he knew he'd been hit. He grimaced and rode out the discomfort as he rolled on the floor, taking Lucilius with him.

Gen heard Mark grunt with pain and knew he'd been hit by whatever magic Garth threw at Lucilius. She was hoping Garth would see the truth, but it seemed he was blinded by his misplaced hate for Lucilius.

Even so, attempting to harm Lucilius was one thing. Hurting Mark was a totally different and unacceptable matter.

Gen felt the nail in her palm throb in sync with her emotions.

Why couldn't humanity believe in the notion of complete repentance? Could someone be so deep in darkness that it's impossible for them to approach the light?

Gen knew she once thought that way, but ever since she was gifted the foot nail, her perception changed. She had hoped to pass that truth on to others, and to a degree, she'd succeeded. Her family believed in her and the message she carried.

But there were people out there who still chose to remain blind, who chose to live in a myopic world where one's future was irredeemable and one's fate unchangeable. Such people were more dangerous than those that walked the corridors of darkness, as these people professed to be something they weren't.

That made Gen angry. Her essence billowed.

"Enough!"

Power burst forth in a circle around her and expanded outward. She felt it wash over everyone in the barn, and for a moment, she experienced the depth of her connection with each of them. She felt Lucilius's remorse and his frustration at his inability to be more useful to the group. As her power healed the wound in Mark's side, she felt the depth of his love and the stability of his faith in her. Gen felt her connection to each member of her family deepen and become stronger as her essence touched the rest of the group. She breathed in Isabella's determination, Josephine's strength, and O'Neal's clarity.

Finally, she saw Garth stagger back as her power hit him. Flashes of images shot through her mind.

A younger-looking Garth sat in what looked like a classroom as an instructor lectured him. Another picture showed a duel between him and a classmate under the supervision of two instructors. There he was, standing before a tombstone, and Gen felt his deep sorrow and grief.

As he recovered his balance, he looked at her in amazement.

"Our past doesn't determine our future, Garth," she said. "Don't let the sorrow of the past shape your future."

Gen knew he had lost someone, and that loss had made him cynical and judgmental.

"And I'll knock out a tooth if you try that stunt again," Mark growled as he got to his feet.

Gen hid a smile. Mark's actions had surprised her. She knew he'd accepted Lucilius begrudgingly—mainly because she'd vouched for the former immortal, but for Mark to sacrifice his life for Lucilius…that was a surprise.

"How stupid can you be?" Mark berated Lucilius as he helped him to his feet. Gen's subtle smile slipped when she saw the fury on Mark's face as he turned back to Garth.

Mark understood Garth's thinking, but that didn't stop the anger welling up within him. Her healing power had taken care of the injury to his side. He felt no more pain; he was invigorated. It was like he'd had a day at a spa followed by a good night's rest.

But none of this quelled his anger. As he strode toward Garth, he saw him begin to cast another spell and was about to knock him senseless when Gen put a gentle hand on his arm.

"It was a mistake, Mark," she said in a soothing voice.

"No, it wasn't. He's still trying to cast a spell as we speak." Mark really wished he had his sword with him. "Don't even think about it," he said, pointing at Garth as he sensed the spell nearing completion.

"Do you understand now, Garth?" Gen asked.

Mark got ready to call on one of his ancestor's memories when he sensed Garth cutting off his spell. The man's demeanour changed, his shoulders slumping in defeat.

"How is that possible?" Garth asked softly.

"That one can change?" Gen replied gently, and he nodded.

Mark waited for a philosophical answer from Gen, but she merely shrugged her shoulders.

"It just is."

Garth found it difficult to accept Gen's truth, but he couldn't deny that something had happened to him.

He hadn't felt any remorse when his needle-shaped shield had struck Mark instead of Lucilius, even though he believed Mark had placed himself in harm's way not by choice but under coercion.

Garth was preparing another attack when Gen's power had hit him, and he'd felt the vastness and purity of the magic that had slammed into his being.

His mind immediately went to Sophia, his fiancée and the only woman he'd ever really loved. Two days before their wedding, she had gone shopping for her "something new." The call Garth had received later destroyed his world.

Sophia had been hit by a drunk driver and died on the way to the hospital. Something had broken in him that day. The last of his remaining belief in justice was eroded when the same drunk driver killed someone else in yet another accident after being paroled early.

People didn't change. They were either good or bad by nature.

From that day onward, Garth had only seen things in black or white, with nothing in between.

He didn't know why Sophia had come to his mind at this moment; she had died over ten years ago, and he told himself he had moved on. But the pain was still fresh in his heart.

"How is that possible?" Garth asked. People couldn't change their nature. The man who killed his fiancée proved that fact. How was it possible that Lucilius, an accursed, could change?

He realized he'd spoken out loud and looked at Gen, needing to know the answer to the question that had laid dormant in his heart for so long. Did his fiancée die in vain? Was it just a random occurrence in the game called life?

"That one can change?" Gen asked softly.

He nodded. "It just is," she said.

The three simple words resonated deep within Garth's soul.

Maybe he would never fully understand the how or the why, but it was true that people could change. A living embodiment of real transformation stood mere feet away from him.

"How...how did it happen?" Garth nodded in Lucilius's direction. He couldn't stand to look at him, but the urge to cast a spell and strike down the accursed had fizzled and become a dying ember.

"That would be a story for him to tell; if and when he chooses," Gen answered.

Garth understood. He could see his mistake clearly now. He had thought the people here were victims of Lucilius's influence, but it was plain to see that Gen was fully in control of her faculties. And her powers...

He had a lot to think about. He eyed the barn door.

"You aren't a prisoner," Gen said. "You can leave any time you want."

He nodded and started for the door when Mark spoke up.

"I trust we won't find you trying to attack any member of this group again."

Garth heard Mark's emphasis on "this group" and nodded.

As he walked out of the barn, he couldn't help but compare the camaraderie he felt amongst the group to the brotherhood of the Citadel.

25

Myrddin snapped awake as cold water splashed in his face. His head still felt sore, but the pounding in his brain had reduced to a bearable degree.

He understood two things as he stared into Marco Brambilla's cold, hard eyes. One, he had been captured by the goons sent to apprehend him in his hotel room. It seemed Marco wanted him alive. The men had entered with guns blazing, yet he was largely unharmed. He was mentally exhausted by the time the second wave of henchmen made it to his room— barely able to stir up the dust on the plush Persian rug, much less summon a tornado. Myrddin had passed out from the numerous fists that had landed on his head, and that brief period of respite had done wonders for his soul.

Yes, his head hurt, and he felt as though he'd been attacked with a baseball bat, but all that pain was superficial and would wash away with a simple healing spell. Surely, they could have killed him.

The second thing he noticed as Marco's eyes blazed in anger was that he was tied up. Thankfully, there weren't any gold obsidian manacles around his wrists this time, and his magic didn't seem to be stifled in any way.

Why would Marco allow him such leeway? Was he so desperate to get his hands back on the crown of thorns that he'd forgotten the advantage his villa provided?

Myrddin heard a groan behind him.

"Is that you, Trosdan?" he asked.

"Who were you expecting, Wizard? Snow White and the seven dwarves?"

Myrddin chuckled. Their situation was dire, but having his magic back, or almost back, made Myrddin more confident of their chances of survival.

"Is the crown safe?" he asked.

"Yes. I hid it, you know where. I felt that would be the best place to keep such an artifact safe."

Myrddin grunted his approval. A pocket dimension was extremely difficult to create and harder still to maintain. The crown would be safe there, and it would take more magic than any being could generate to penetrate the ethereal dimension.

"Where are we?" Trosdan asked.

Myrddin looked around. He gazed past Marco, who, for the moment, seemed content to glare quietly from his seat. They seemed to be in some sort of warehouse, and the distant sound of splashing suggested that they were close to a body of water.

"Why are we just standing around like confused characters in a cheap movie?" a female voice barked harshly, and Candice stepped out of the shadows.

"Where is the relic?" she demanded as she loomed over Myrddin.

"Hey, be careful with that one," Trosdan warned. "The broad is crazy. She shot me three times."

Myrddin ignored Candice and reached out with his essence to ascertain what kind of numbers they were up against. He sensed a few men waiting outside the warehouse, most of them armed.

"I don't get it, Marco," Myrddin said. "Why bring us here? This place serves you no advantage."

Marco ignored the question, but Myrddin was content to wait. Based on their past interactions, he believed the giant would be itching to tell the world his super smart plan any minute now.

He didn't have to wait long.

Marco got up from his chair and strode toward Myrddin. He was still wearing the same dusty suit. Myrddin guessed having your attire reinforced with gold obsidian must cost an arm and a leg.

"You magicians think you are so smart," Marco drawled. "You rely too much on your magic and not enough on your natural, God-given talents. My men are on their way right now with a weapon that would kill even you, Wizard."

Myrddin frowned. His magic was a God-given, natural talent, but he didn't think Marco would find it amusing to be corrected about that.

And a weapon that could kill him? That could only mean something covered in more gold obsidian.

Candice moved back when Marco had approached Myrddin; she was still intimidated by the giant.

"Have you rested enough?" Trosdan asked from behind Myrddin.

"Come on; you could have waited a few more minutes for him to spill any secrets we may need to know," Myrddin hissed at his friend.

Marco snarled and reached out, but Myrddin was tired of playing possum. He generated a shield of solid air, which Marco's fist slammed into. Trosdan roared behind Myrddin as he ripped through the binds, pushed himself up, and slammed his feet into Marco's chest. As expected, the kick didn't hurt Marco, but the force sent Myrddin flying back from the huge man.

As he landed, he sliced through Trosdan's remaining bonds with a blade of air and floated gently to his feet. Trosdan hurried to his side.

"So, it has come to this, Wizard," Marco said. "My strength against your magic. We shall see who triumphs tonight." A maniacal grin spread across his face, and Myrddin snapped a shield of essence into place around his body.

Was this what the crime boss was after? A battle on neutral ground to find out who was greater?

"We don't have to do a thing, Marco. We can still part ways amicably."

"You are not leaving here alive, Merlin, if it means burning this building down with you in it."

Myrddin noticed Candice begin to gather her essence, the air around her palms igniting in orbs of fire.

"How do you want to play this?" Trosdan asked warily.

Myrddin couldn't blame the stout fellow; Marco and Candice were formidable opponents. On his own, Myrddin didn't like his chances of winning, but with Trosdan by his side, the odds were tilted in their favour. Especially as they still had one trump card left to play.

He was sure neither Marco nor Candice knew of the edge Trosdan had over everyone in the warehouse.

"I know some of my past actions and decisions have been questionable, but you can't be that old for me to have slighted you. What perceived harm do you feel I've caused you?" Myrddin asked Candice.

"Perceived harm?" Candice screamed. "That's all you can say after everything you've done to my family? You are a fraud, and you only use people until they are of no more value to you."

"Who are you?" he asked softly. It was obvious Candice carried the weight of a significant grievance over something Myrddin had done, but the wizard couldn't think when or how it could have happened.

Candice laughed bitterly. "My name is Candice Blackburn, descendant of Morgana Blackburn, daughter of Derog the Great."

Derog the Banished!

Myrddin reeled back in shock.

"I see you recognize the name, Merlin," she spat. "You destroyed a young man because you had more power than him. But guess what? He outsmarted you. You broke his channels for magic but not his knowledge of it."

"He made a grimoire," Myrddin gasped, suddenly realizing. That was the only way Derog could have passed on his dark knowledge.

"Your ancestor wasn't the saint you think him to be, Candice. He practiced dark magic and human sacrifice. He summoned demons to this realm. He needed to be stopped."

"Liar!"

Candice hurled two fireballs at Myrddin, but he swatted them aside with his air magic. It seemed the time for talking was over.

Trosdan didn't like to fight. He knew his mutation gave him an edge, and his destructive anger couldn't ever be allowed to get out of hand, so he entered the fray half-heartedly, charging at Marco. The man grinned sadistically and swiped at him with a giant hand. Trosdan crossed his arms and protected his head as Marco's fist crashed down on him. For the

302

first time in decades, Trosdan felt pain vibrate down his arms as the force of the punch took him down.

The giant ignored him and rushed at Myrddin, who created another shield of hardened air. What Myrddin didn't see was Marco slipping on his gold obsidian knuckle dusters. Trosdan yelled out a warning, but he knew it was too late. Marco shattered Myrddin's shield with a single swing of his fist.

The wizard restored his shield and turned to engage Marco again, leaving his back open for Candice to hurl another fireball at him. The flames washed over his shield in a shower of red sparks. The shield flickered blue, but it held.

Marco swung back for another strike, and Trosdan knew his friend's shield wouldn't hold. Marco intended to kill Myrddin, and the unfairness of the fight angered Trosdan greatly.

Screaming with rage, he rushed at the giant.

Ever since the fight on his balcony, Marco had been in a heightened state of euphoria. The desire to crush the wizard and show everyone around that he was the alpha predator overwhelmed him as he smashed through Myrddin's shield with his knuckle dusters.

The wizard turned to face him, and Marco grinned in anticipation of the agony he would soon inflict. He would beat the old man within an inch of his life before extracting the information he needed. Only then would the wizard have a date with the fishes. He chose the warehouse for that singular purpose.

Marco wanted to scream in frustration when Candice threw her fireballs at Myrddin but breathed a sigh of relief when the attack washed over the wizard without any effect. It seemed Myrddin had already shaped another shield, but it would not hold against the gold obsidian.

He swung back his fist as he gathered energy for his next punch. He knew his strength was uncanny. Nothing and no one could withstand his fists— including Myrddin's shield—not against the gold obsidian.

His fist sailed through toward the wizard, and Marco braced himself for impact. But, to his surprise, his arm jerked to a halt mid-air. Marco looked down to see the little man, Trosdan, holding on to his elbow. The man's grip barely covered Marco's bulky arm, but somehow, it rendered him immovable.

"What sorcery is this?" he uttered in disbelief.

He shrugged out of Trosdan's grip and faced him.

"You think you can take me, little man?" he sneered.

The man looked up at Marco, his eyes glowing red.

"You do not hurt my friends."

Trosdan drew back his arm and swung at the giant. Marco's contemptuous sneer slipped as Trosdan's fist connected with his stomach. He grunted in pain and fell to one knee.

Non è possibile!

Marco heard a loud crack and, for a second, wondered where the sound had come from. The pain igniting his arm quickly made it clear that his elbow had shattered.

He tried to get to his feet, but the little man was like an avenging angel—or a destructive demon. Punches rained down incessantly. He tried his best to block them, but each blow was like being hit by a jackhammer. As Marco slipped into unconsciousness, he realized, for the first time, that there were forces in the world that wielded greater power than him.

Myrddin turned his full attention to Candice as Trosdan engaged Marco in battle. The young girl had courage and would have made an excellent disciple, but her anger and hatred made her spells sloppy and easy to dodge. He allowed the next fireball to sail harmlessly across his shielded face as he advanced toward her.

"You still have a chance to turn back from this path, young woman. Don't be like your ancestor."

"You are a liar, Merlin. I have studied and waited for this moment. My plan is to make you endure what you inflicted on me. To watch your family suffer as mine did."

Myrddin easily caught the next ball of fire and extinguished the flames by clenching his fist.

The attack was a feign as Candice chanted and raised her palm towards Myrddin. She blew dust particles as she made an incantation. The particles flashed like ignited gunpowder but gave out a deep yellow illuminance. The glow grew, and Myrddin watched as the particles solidified into the shape of a large bird – albeit one that was on fire.

Transference, and on a very high level.

A part of Myrddin dipped his head in respect to the young woman fighting him. He could count on one hand, the number of people that could accomplish such a feat. The young girl was truly talented. A shame she was as deranged as her ancestor.

The bird screeched, snapping Myrddin's attention back to the moment. It stood close to seven feet and glared down at Myrddin. He saw the same hate in its eyes as the person that had conjured it. The bird attacked, trying to peck Myrddin but meeting his shield instead.

Candice had retreated to the other side of the warehouse, probably trying to get her essence back.

That was the thing with this kind of power display. It took a truckload of essence to make your essence visible and give it a will of its own. A giant fiery bird would have been a problem for some people but not someone that could manipulate different types of essence. And especially not someone like him.

Myrddin locked the bird down with a whip of air.

'Duratus!' Myrddin voiced out.

Nothing happened at first, but Myrddin could sense the command giving birth as the ground around the burning bird began to show glittering tiny ice shards. The bird struggled in Myrddin's air whip, sensing its doom approaching, but Myrddin held it down with his will. The ice shards grew, becoming frost as it crept up the fiery bird's feet. In less than a minute, the bird was transformed to a large ice sculpture.

'Confractus.' It was a command to shatter in Latin, and the ice essence that had merged with the bird obeyed. Myrddin walked towards Candice as the bird shattered into tiny pieces, Myrddin's shield protecting him from the blast.

Candice watched her fiery bird blew up, and she prepared her next attack. This was a day etched in Candice's mind. She knew her power was inconsequential when compared with Myrddin's. The wizard could squash her like a bug in a full-frontal confrontation, but Candice had no intention of testing her might against Myrddin.

Candice couldn't beat Myrddin one-on-one, but that was if she wasn't prepared. Candice steadied her breathing and touched one of the rings on her fingers. A rush of essence flooded her soul, and the ring disintegrated into dust. Candice grimaced. The ring had cost her a truckload of cash and hours of deep meditation to store a reserve of essence.

Candice created more orbs of fire and lobbed them at Myrddin. The wizard barely flinched as the orbs hit his shield and did nothing. Candice wasn't deterred. Her plan wasn't to hurt him with the orbs but to cause him to move. Candice drained the remaining essence she'd gathered from the ring in a torrent of blazing fire that she aimed at Myrddin. She saw the shield around Myrddin strengthen as the wizard poured essence into it. Myrddin didn't see that the blast's force had pushed him backward – to the area Candice wanted him to be.

Candice smiled internally. Her powers may not equal Myrddin's, but tonight, she would bring down a titan.

Myrddin was surprised when he felt a surge of essence enter Candice. He saw the trail of essence leave the ring and enter the young woman's body. Myrddin took a moment to study the rings on her fingers. The woman had a ring on each finger, and each glowed with power.

A stream of fire shot toward Myrddin, and he strengthened his shield. The blast washed over his shield, but the force pushed him back.

Again, Myrddin had to respect the young woman's ingenuity and resolve. Myrddin staggered back when he heard a clang and the air around him tightened.

That couldn't be good.

Myrddin felt essence rush out of him in an alarming rate. He followed the flow of power and saw a large and complex sigil carved on the warehouse's roof.

Ingenious.

'Solvite!' Myrddin worked quickly. He released a huge amount of essence into the glowing sigil and overloaded the construct. There was a whoosh as the sigil broke, and a rush of air buffeted the four fighters in the warehouse.

Myrddin fell to a knee as weakness washed over him. The sigil and expended essence had taken a lot from him. The constructed sigil was two-way, and Myrddin saw Candice standing in a similar circle. So Myrddin wasn't surprised when the stolen essence funneled into Candice's body.

Not good. Not good at all.

Power rushed into Candice at an alarming rate. Her body shook, and the rings on her fingers glowed brightly. Candice screamed in ecstasy as she took all the stolen essence in. It was more than she'd ever felt in her life, but she swallowed the pain and imbibed all the spell gave. The rings on her fingers cracked as excess power engulfed them. Candice willed the essence from the broken rings back into her body. She needed all the power she could gather.

Essence caused the air around her to spark and sizzle. Candice's gaze fell on Myrddin, and she sensed the glimmer of apprehension in them.

Time to kill a titan.

Trosdan gave as much as he received. He was battered and bruised, one eye swollen shut, and what looked like a couple of broken ribs made breathing difficult. Marco wasn't any better. A fist had connected with the giant's face and Trosdan was glad to see the protrusion of flesh marking a bruise on Marco's face.

'You are nothing. You will fall.' Marco spat at Trosdan. Trosdan didn't bother replying, conserving his energy and allowing his fists do the talking. The giant had height advantage over Trosdan, but the stout man had greater punching power—that and a skin that would put any armor to shame.

Trosdan dodged another punch and stepped into Marco's guard. He was on his last fumes; they both were, and they both knew it. The fight would soon be over. Marco threw another punch, hoping to distance himself from Trosdan. However, he understood he had greater reach and did more damage from a distance. The reverse was true for Trosdan, who needed to get close to deliver his punches.

Trosdan took Marco's punch with his head, grunting in pain at the impact. It was a surprising move and one Trosdan hoped would give him the advantage. Trosdan smiled in satisfaction when he heard a crack as Marco's wrist snapped.

He bellowed as he tackled Marco by the waist, and in an amazing show of inhuman power, Trosdan lifted the giant and slammed him on the floor.

The fight was over as Trosdan rained punches on the dazed man beneath him.

Myrddin didn't think but allowed instincts and reflexes garnered from hundreds of years to take over. He clapped his palms together as he sensed Candice building up an attack. He wove air, lacing it with earth and wind. A shield appeared in his front. Runes covered the face of the shimmering blue shield.

The Buckler of Aegis.

It was a desperate move he hadn't done in a long time, but Myrddin believed the situation was dire. The power Candice was channeling would rip through his normal shields like a laser beam cutting paper. He needed something that could save him from being obliterated.

Myrddin channeled all the will to live into the shield as Candice blasted him with all the gathered power she'd summoned. Candice's essence hit Myrddin's created shield, and the warehouse was immersed in white light. The earth shook, and power blasted into the air. The power hit the waters around the warehouse and drove them back, exposing the bare earth at the bottom of the river. With a rumble, the waters filled back, splashing the buildings around the harbor.

Myrddin gritted his teeth, allowing the pain of clenching them to fuel his will. He remembered his goal and his purpose and planted his feet firmer on the ground. His body shook in pain as Candice spell sought to consume his shield and wipe him from the face of the earth.

The beam of destruction shut off as quickly as it had struck and Myrddin sighed in relief.

He lived.

Myrddin allowed the Buckler of Aegis to dissipate. It had taken all of his remaining essence to summon and maintain the spell. He looked up to see the grin on Candice's face and another beam of power shot out of the young woman. Myrddin rose his hand and summoned another shield but knew it wouldn't be enough to stop the path of death heading towards him.

The feedback from Candice's spell threw Trosdan across the warehouse. He tumbled and hit the wall with a groan. He felt like pulverized meat. He saw Myrddin trying to hold his own against the power beating against his shield.

The Buckler of Aegis.

Trosdan hadn't seen the wizard pull out that spell in a long time. That could only mean that things were desperate for his friend. Trosdan struggled to his feet. He had to help his friend. Gathering his flagging strength, Trosdan ran towards the fight between Myrddin and Candice.

Candice was winning. She couldn't believe it. She had planned for it, prepared as much as she could but seeing it happen before her eyes was surprising.

Containing this much power would tell on her body and spirit but Candice was willing to pay the price if it meant the death of Myrddin.

She would have revenge.

The attack wore out and Candice saw Myrddin still on his feet. Myrddin was spent, and Candice basked in the moment. She was also at her last reserve, but she would drain every ounce of essence if she had to. She could taste victory and she smiled.

All she had to do was channel another destructive energy at the wizard.

This ends now.

Candice felt the pull of the spell as the energy sucked out all the essence in her soul. She felt light-headed but shook of the feeling of weakness. She would watch with her last dying breath as Myrddin died by her hands.

Candice heard footsteps rushing towards her.

No! Nothing will snatch this moment from her. She poured more into the spell and felt something break within her soul. Candice screamed in agony as she released the spell. Myrddin must die.

Trosdan didn't have a moment to ponder his intentions as he reached Myrddin. The wizard had fallen to a knee and had a palm stretched out before him. Trosdan sensed his friend trying to build a defense against the destructive power raging towards him. Whatever Myrddin hoped to do wouldn't work as

Trosdan felt the difference in power between the incoming attack and Myrddin's shield.

Trosdan wrapped his friend in his arms, covering the tired wizard with his body. The spell hit Trosdan – and did nothing.

The destructive essence washed over Trosdan and hit the wall. It blew a huge hole and shot into the vast body of water behind the warehouse. Trosdan turned and saw Candice sprawled on the floor.

'We need to get out of here.' Trosdan said as he helped Myrddin to his feet. Myrddin struggled to his feet to walked towards Candice's body.

'I don't think she's alive.' Trosdan hadn't felt anything from the young woman.

'She's alive.' Myrddin said with a tired breath. He looked exhausted and worn out.

'What have you done to my family?' Myrddin growled. Trosdan watched as Myrddin tried to create his signature whip of air but failed.

'Tell me child, and maybe you will get to live to see another dawn.'

'You think you are invincible? You believe no one can touch you? Well, guess again.'

'We need to get out of here, Myrddin,' Trosdan cautioned. He could feel the anger in Myrddin as the wizard struggled to quell his rioting emotions and shoved his anger back. Candice crawled to the closest wall and sat with her back leaning against the wall.

'It's already in motion, Merlin. People will hate and despise your granddaughter for who she is, just like you made sure my ancestor became a pariah.' Candice stared at Myrddin, 'The world will know, and what you've tried to hide for so long will come to light. She will be branded a heretic and a practitioner of evil.' A malicious smile twisted Candice's face as she slumped back against the wall. Trosdan could see that her brief outburst had taken a lot out of her.

'I can see that the apple didn't fall far from the tree. You are every bit as vile as Derog. Derog was evil. He craved power and didn't care how many people that got hurt. You don't have to follow that same path.'

'You are full of lies. Today, I showed that you aren't the god you claim to be. You can die just as we mere mortals.'

'I never claimed to be what I am not. There is only one true God, Candice. You have a twisted version of what actually happened. Ask yourself this – why are you still alive? If I'm the kind of person you have been taught to believe, why haven't I killed you?'

'You are as spent as I am.'

'No, Candice. You passed a threshold. Do you feel that ache in your spirit? Your quest for vengeance came with a price, and I pray you can live with the cost.'

Trosdan frowned and studied the woman before him. He saw her try to breathe calmly but struggle to maintain her breathing quality. Trosdan pushed the concern for the woman to the back of his mind. She would live; that was all that mattered – right.

'What have you done to me?' Candice asked as tears ran down her cheeks.

'I didn't do anything to you; you did this to yourself.' Myrddin replied.

Trosdan took as much of his friend's weight as possible as they staggered towards the exit.

Marco's men stared in silence as Myrddin and Trosdan emerged from the burning warehouse. No one attempted to stop the duo as they walked away.

"You said I wouldn't have to get angry," Trosdan grumbled, but Myrddin could tell his friend's heart wasn't in it.

"I also promised you a good story to tell your grandkids," he replied with a chuckle.

"Now that's over, don't call me for the next decade or two."

"Things are happening, Trosdan. My family is going to need your help very soon. The forces of darkness are gathering."

Trosdan merely grunted, a response Myrddin knew was begrudging consent.

Myrddin massaged his temples and closed his eyes. He was tired, so tired, but he knew he wouldn't rest until he returned to the Triple 7 ranch.

26

Gen was leaning against the porch railing, watching Lucilius hold the broken door frame in place while Mark reattached the hinges.

"Do you think it will hold? she asked.

"At least until we get a new one," Mark answered.

"People will begin to wonder what's happening here. This will be the second door we've ordered in a few months."

As the two men worked, Gen kept glancing at the entrance of the Triple 7 ranch. Her granddad had called to tell her he would be taking the next flight back, and she was excited for his return.

She grinned as she imagined his face when she would tell him of everything that happened during his absence and how her bond with the foot nail had deepened. She heard a vehicle approaching and leaned forward in anticipation, but it wasn't him.

A bronco jeep drove into the ranch with four men standing at the back.

"Go back to hell where you belong, Witch!" one of them yelled. Gen watched in amazement as the man threw a Molotov cocktail at the barn. The men whooped with delight as it caught fire.

Mark rushed to Gen's side, then took a step toward the men, but she held him back.

"Don't. It will only make things worse." She had spotted the man in the passenger seat holding a phone and recording.

"We can't let them get away with this!" Lucilius growled, but Mark shook his head; he must have seen the man recording, too.

The front door swayed on its hinges as the rest of the group flocked outside.

"What's going on?" Josephine asked.

"This is what I was afraid of," Isabella said with a tremble in her voice.

"Russell Patel's podcasts," Gen affirmed. "People's fears are going to be whipped up. This could be the beginning of something nasty."

"We won't let anything harm any of us," Mark said.

"How are you going to do that without looking like the bad guys? They're hoping we'll retaliate so their actions can be justified," Isabella said.

"So, what do we do?" Josephine asked, her brow furrowed in frustration.

Gen watched the jubilating men with sorrow in her heart.

How could mankind be so blind?

With a final whoop, the men turned the car around and drove out of sight, the barn blazing behind them.

"Can you reverse the damage?" Mark asked Josephine.

"Sorry, I can only reverse the flow of time for a minute or two. Anything longer than that wouldn't work."

"But we can at least douse the fire," Mark ventured.

"How do we do that?" Gen asked. The flames were too high for them to fight by themselves, and the town's fire department consisted of a water truck and volunteers from the community. The barn would be gone by the time help arrived.

The group stared in horror as the flames licked the roof and, with a resounding crash, the entire barn collapsed.

"Do you think they'll be back?" Josephine asked.

"Most likely. I think we need to tell Theo about this," Gen reasoned. People like the men in the jeep would keep pushing and shoving until they were stopped, and she believed the police would be best placed to handle matters.

The group was so caught up in the spectacle of the fire that they didn't hear another vehicle approaching.

Mark was the first to notice, and Gen followed his gaze when she saw a smile lighting up his face.

Her granddad was back.

A taxi stopped in the driveway, and Myrddin got out. Gen ran into his open arms and felt his reassuring embrace surround her.

"What's going on here?" Myrddin asked.

"Welcome back, Myrddin. Great timing. Except, you missed the fireworks by a couple of minutes," Mark said, patting him on the back.

Myrddin didn't like what he'd just heard.

The whole group was in the sitting room, filling him in on everything that had been happening. It seemed Candice had done more damage than he had thought.

Yesterday, he had been elated to hear that everyone was safe. But considering what had just taken place, things were clearly not okay. He was glad Gen had advocated a non-violent approach, as these types of situations could easily escalate until someone got seriously hurt.

"What do you guys think about moving?" Myrddin asked casually, hoping to gauge the group's reactions.

The idea occurred to him during the flight back to Canada, but he'd hoped to discuss it with Gen and Mark alone first.

Myrddin looked around. Gen was frowning, and Isabella and Josephine looked confused. Mark's stoic expression showed he had clearly already read the situation, and Lucilius's blank look was inscrutable.

O'Neal merely gave Myrddin a calculating look, also not giving anything away.

"What do you mean, Granddad?" Gen finally asked.

"What do you say about moving somewhere bigger?" he asked.

"Sorry, but I don't think there's anywhere in this town that's bigger than the ranch," Josephine answered.

"That's true, young woman," Myrddin laughed softly.

"Outside of Dundurn, he means," Mark said.

Myrddin nodded, and he could see the lights go on in the minds of the people gathered around the sitting room.

"Leave Dundurn? Are you sure, Granddad?"

"Very sure, Gen. Truth be told, I think it's about time."

"But where would we go?"

"Vancouver isn't so bad," Isabella said with a smile.

"No, let's head to Toronto. I've always wanted to go there," Josephine countered.

Myrddin saw they were waiting for him to make a suggestion, but he remained silent.

"You're not thinking of Canada, are you, Granddad?" Gen frowned as the notion dawned on her. "What about mum and dad?" she added, her face filled with concern.

"Moving far away would be the best option, Gen," Mark said. Myrddin could tell he understood the reasons behind the suggestion to move.

"With you out of the country, the protesters have nothing to protest. Your parents would be safer too," Mark continued.

Myrddin gave them a moment to digest the concept before addressing the group again.

"What do you think about moving to England?"

END

Made in the USA
Coppell, TX
26 May 2024

32820462R00184